Sabine Baring-Gould

Cheap Jack Zita

Vol. 1

Sabine Baring-Gould

Cheap Jack Zita
Vol. 1

ISBN/EAN: 9783337324711

Printed in Europe, USA, Canada, Australia, Japan

Cover: Foto ©Andreas Hilbeck / pixelio.de

More available books at **www.hansebooks.com**

CHEAP JACK ZITA

BY

S. BARING GOULD

AUTHOR OF

'MEHALAH' 'URITH' 'IN THE ROAR OF THE SEA
'MRS. CURGENVEN' ETC.

IN THREE VOLUMES

VOLUME I

Methuen & Co.
18 BURY STREET, LONDON, W.C.
1893

CONTENTS OF VOL. I

CHEAP JACK ZITA

CHAPTER I

BEFORE THE GALILEE

WHAT was the world coming to? The world — the centre of it — the Isle of Ely?

What aged man in his experience through threescore years and ten had heard of such conduct before?

What local poet, whose effusions appeared in the 'Cambridge and Ely Post,' in his wildest flights of imagination, conceived of such a thing?

Decency must have gone to decay and been

buried. Modesty must have unfurled her wings
and sped to heaven before such an event could
become possible.

Where were the constables? Were bye-laws
to become dead letters? Were order, propriety
the eternal fitness of things, to be trampled
under foot by vagabonds?

In front of the cathedral, before the Galilee,
—the magnificent west porch of the minster of
St. Etheldreda,—a Cheap Jack's van was drawn
up.

Within twenty yards of the Bishop's palace,
where every word uttered was audible in every
room, a Cheap Jack was offering his wares.

Effrontery was, in heraldic language, rampant
and regardant.

A crowd was collected about the van; a
crowd composed of all sorts and conditions
of men, jostling each other, trampling on the
grass of the lawn, climbing up the carved work
of the cathedral, to hear, to see, to bid, to buy.

Divine service was hardly over. The organ was still mumbling and tooting, when through the west door came a drift of choristers, who had flung off their surplices and had raced down the nave, that they might bid against and out-bid each other for the pocket-knives offered by Cheap Jack.

Mr. Faggs, the beadle, was striding in the same direction, relaxing the muscles of his face from the look of severe ecclesiastical solemnity into which they were drawn during divine worship. It had occurred to him during the singing of the anthem that there were sundry articles of domestic utility Cheap Jack was selling that it might be well for him to secure at a low figure.

Mr. Bowles, the chief bailiff, had come forth from evensong with his soul lifted up with thankfulness that he was not as other men were : he attended the cathedral daily, he subscribed to all the charities ; and now he stood looking on, his breath taken away, his feet riveted to the soil by surprise at the audacity of the Cheap Jack, in daring to draw up before the minster, and vend his wares during the hour of afternoon prayer.

The servant maids in the canons' houses in the Close had their heads craned out from such narrow Gothic windows as would allow their brachycephalic skulls to pass, and were listening and lawk-a-mussying and oh-mying over the bargains.

Nay, the Bishop himself was in an upper room, the window-sash of which was raised, ensconced behind the curtain, with his ear open and cocked, and he was laughing at what he heard till his apron rippled, his bald head waxed pink, and his calves quivered.

Very little of the sides of the van was visible, so encrusted were they with brooms, brushes, door-mats, tin goods, and coalscuttles. Between these articles might be detected the glimmer of

the brimstone yellow of the carcase of the shop
on wheels. The front of the conveyance was
open; it was festooned with crimson plush
curtains, drawn back; and, deep in its depths
could be discerned racks and ranges of shelves,
stored with goods of the most various and
inviting description.

The front of the van was so contrived as to
fall forward, and in so falling to disengage a pair
of supports that sustained it, and temporarily
converted it into a platform. On this platform
stood the Cheap Jack, a gaunt man with bushy
dark hair and sunken cheeks; he was speaking
with a voice rendered hoarse by bellowing. He
was closely shaven. He wore drab breeches and
white stockings, a waistcoat figured with flowers,
and was in his shirt sleeves. On his head was
a plush cap, with flaps that could be turned up
or down as occasion served. When turned down,
that in front was converted into a peak that
sheltered his eyes, those at the sides protected

his ears, and that behind prevented rain from coursing down the nape of his neck. When, however, these four lappets were turned up, they transformed the cap into a crown—a crown such as it behoved the King of Cheap Jacks to wear. The man was pale and sallow, sweat-drops stood on his brow, and it was with an effort that he maintained the humour with which he engaged the attention of his hearers, and that he made his voice audible to those in the outermost ring of the curious and interested clustered about the van. Within, in the shadowed depths of the conveyance, glimpses were obtained of a girl, who moved about rapidly and came forward occasionally to hand the Cheap Jack such articles as he demanded, or to receive from him such as had failed to command a purchaser.

When she appeared, it was seen that she was a slender, well-built girl of about seventeen summers, with ripe olive skin, a thick head of short-cut chestnut hair, and a pair of hazel eyes.

Apparently she was unmoved by her father's jokes; they provoked no smile on her lips, for they were familiar to her; and she was equally unmoved by the admiration she aroused among the youths, with which also she was apparently familiar.

'Here now!' shouted the Cheap Jack. 'What the dickens have I got?—a spy-glass to be sure, and such a spy-glass as never was and never will be offered again. When I was a-comin' along the road from Cambridge, and was five miles off, "Tear and ages!" sez I, seein' your famous cathedral standin' up in the sunshine,—"Tear and ages!" sez I; "that's a wonder of the world." And I up wi' my spy-glass. Now look here. You observe as 'ow one of the western wings be fallen down. 'Tis told that when the old men built up that there top storey to the tower, that it throwed the left wing down. Now I looked through this perspective glass, and I seed both wings standing just as they used to be, and just as they ought to be, but ain't. I couldn't take less than seventeen and six for this here wonderful spy-glass—seventeen and six. What! not buy a glass as will show you how things ought to be, but ain't?' He turned to the circle round him from side to side. 'Come now,—say ten shillings. 'Tis a shame to take the perspective glass out of Ely.' A pause. 'No one inclined to bid ten shillings? Take it back, Zita. These here Ely folk be that poor they can't go above tenpence. Ten shillings soars above their purses. But stay. Zita, give me that there glass again. There is something more than is wonderful about it. You look through and you'll see what's to your advantage, and that's what every one don't see wi' the naked eye. Come—say seven shillings!'

No bid.

'And let me tell the ladies—they've but to look through, and they'll see the *him* they've set their 'arts on, comin', comin',—bloomin' as a rose, and 'olding the wedding ring in 'is 'and.'

In went the heads of the servant maids of the canons' residences.

'I say!' shouted one of the choristers, 'will it show us a coming spanking?'

'Of course it will,' answered the Cheap Jack, 'because it's to your advantage.'

'Let us look then.'

Cheap Jack handed the telescope to the lad. He put his eye to it, drew the glass out, lowered it, and shouted, 'I see nothing.'

'Of course not. You're such a darlin' good boy; you ain't going to have no spanking.'

'Let me look,' said a shop-girl standing by.

Cheap Jack waited. Every one watched.

'I don't see nothing,' said the girl.

'Of course not. You ain't got a sweetheart, and never will have one.'

A roar of laughter, and the young woman retired in confusion.

'And, I say,' observed the boy, as he returned the glass, 'it's all a cram about the fallen transept. I looked, and saw it was down.'

'Of course you did,' retorted the Cheap Jack. 'Didn't I say five miles off? Go five miles along the Wisbeach Road, and you'll see it sure enough, as I said. There—five shillings for it.'

'I'll give you half a crown.'

'Half a crown!' jeered the vendor. 'There, though, you're a quirister, and for the sake o' your beautiful voice, and because you're such a good boy, as don't deserve nor expect a whacking, you shall have it for half a crown.'

The Bishop's nose and one eye were thrust from behind the curtain.

'Why,' said the Right Reverend to himself, 'that's Tom Bulk, as mischievous a young rogue as there is in the choir and grammar school. He is as sure of a caning this week as —as'—

'Thanky, sir,' said Cheap Jack, pocketing the half-crown. 'Zita, what next? Hand me that blazin' crimson plush weskit.'

From out the dark interior stepped the girl, and the sunshine flashed over her, lighting her auburn hair, rich as burnished copper. She wore a green, scarlet, and yellow flowered kerchief, tied across her bosom, and knotted behind her back. Bound round her waist was a white apron.

She deigned no glance at the throng, but kept her eyes fixed on her father's face.

'Are you better, dad?' she asked in a low tone.

'Not much, Zit. But I'll go through with it.'

'Here we are now!' shouted the Jack, after he had drawn the sleeve of his left arm across his brow and lips, that were bathed in perspiration. And yet the weather was cold; the season was the end of October, and the occasion of the visit of the van to Ely was Tawdry (St. Etheldreda's) Fair.

A whisper and nudges passed among the young men crowded about the van.

' Ain't she just a stunner?'

' I say, I wish the Cheap Jack would put up the girl to sale.   Wouldn't there be bidding?'

' She's the finest thing about the caravan.'

Such were comments that flew from one to another.

' Now, then!' bellowed the vendor of cheap wares; 'here you are again! A red velvet weskit, with splendid gold—real gold—buttons. You shall judge; I'll put it on.'

The man suited the action to the word. Then he straightened his legs and arms, and turned himself about from side to side to exhibit the full beauty of the vestment from every quarter.

' Did you ever see the like of this?' he shouted. 'But them breeches o' mine have a sort o' deadening effect on the beauty of the weskit.

Thirty shillings is the price. You should see it along with a black frock-coat and black trousers. Then it's glorious! It's something you can wear with just what you likes. No one looks at rags when you've this on, so took up is they with the weskit. What is that you said, sir? Twenty-five shillings was your offer? It is yours—and all because I sees it'll go with them great black whiskers of yours like duck and green peas. It'll have a sort of a mellering effect on their bushiness, and 'armonise with them as well as the orging goes wi' the chanting of the quiristers.'

Jack handed the waistcoat, which he had hastily plucked off his back, to one of the lay-clerks of the cathedral. The man turned as red as the waistcoat, and thrust his hands behind his back.

'I never bid for it,' he protested.

'Beg pardon, sir; I thought you nodded your 'ead to me, but it was the wind a-blowin' of it

about. That gentleman with the black flowin'
whiskers don't take the weskit; it is still for
sale. I'll let you have it for fifteen shillings,
and it'll make you a conquering hero among
the females. You, sir? Here you are.'

He addressed the chief bailiff, Mr. Bowles,
an elderly, white-whiskered, semi-clerical official,
the pink and paragon of propriety.

'No!' exclaimed Cheap Jack, as Mr. Bowles,
with unlifted palms and averted head, staggered
back. 'No—his day is past. But I can see by
the twinkle of his eye he was the devil among
the gals twenty years ago. It's the young chaps
who must compete for the weskit. I'll tell you
something rare,' continued the man, after clear-
ing his throat and mopping his brow and lips.
'No one will think but what you're a lord or a
harchbishop when you 'ave this 'ere weskit on.
As I was a-coming into Ely in this here concern,
sez I to myself, "I'll put on an appearance out
o' respect to this ancient and venerable city."

So I drawed on this weskit; and what should 'appen but we meets his most solemn and sacred lordship, the Bishop of the diocese.'

'This is coming it rather strong,' said the person alluded to behind the curtain, and his face and head became hot and damp.

'Well, and when his lordship, the Right Reverend, saw me, he lifted up his holy eyes and looked at my weskit. And then sez he to himself, "Lawk-a-biddy, it's the Prince!" and down he went in the dirt afore me, grovellin' with his nose in the mire. He did, upon my word.'

'Upon my word, this is monstrous! this is insufferable! A joke is a joke!' gasped the Bishop, very much agitated. 'There's modera-tion in all things—a limitation to be observed even in exaggeration. I haven't been on the Wisbeach Road this fortnight. I never saw the man. I never went down in the dirt. This is positively appalling!

He took a turn round the room, went to the bell, then considered that it would be inadvisable to summon the footman and show that he had been listening to the nonsense of a Cheap Jack. Accordingly he went back to the window, hid himself once more behind the curtain, but so trembled with excitement and distress, that the whole curtain trembled with him.

'Nine and six. Here you are. Nine and six for this splendid garment, and cheap it is—dirt cheap. You're a lucky man, sir; and won't you only cut out your rivals with the darling?'

Cheap Jack handed the plush waistcoat to a young farmer from the Fens; then suddenly he turned himself about, looked into his van, and said in a husky voice—

'Zit, I can't go yarning no longer. I've got to the end of my powers; you carry on.'

'Right, father; I'm the boy for you with the general public.'

The man stepped within. As he did so, the

girl lowered one of the curtains so as to conceal
him.   He sank wearily on a bench at the side.
She stooped with a quivering lip and filling eye
and kissed him, then sprang forward and stood
outside on the platform, contemplating the
crowd with a look of assurance, mingled with
contempt.

CHAPTER II

THE FLAILS

'NOW, here's a chance you may never have again—a chance, let me tell you, you never *will* have again.' She extended in both hands packages of tea done up in silvered paper. ' The general public gets cheated in tea—it does —tremenjous! It is given sloe leaves, all kinds of rubbish, and pays for it a fancy price. Father, he has gone and bought a plantation out in China, and has set over it a real mandarin with nine tails, and father guarantees that this tea is the very best of our plantation teas, and he sells it at a price which puts it within the reach of all. Look here!' she turned a parcel about ; 'here you are, with the mandarin's own seal upon it, to let every one know it is genuine, and that it is the only genuine tea sent over.'

'Where's the plantation, eh, girl?' jeered a boy from the grammar school.

'Where is it?' answered the girl, turning sharply on her interlocutor. 'It's at Fumchoo. Do you know where Fumchoo is? You don't? and yet you sets up to be a scholar. It is fifteen miles from Pekin by the high road, and seven and a half over the fields. Go to school and look at your map, and tell your master he ought to be ashamed of himself not to ha' made you know your geography better. Now, then, here's your chance. Finest orange-flower Pekoe at four shillings. Beat that if you can.' No offers. 'I am not coming down in my price. Don't think that; not a farthing. Four shillings a pound; but I'll try to meet you in another way. I keep the tea in quarter-pound parcels as well. Perhaps that'll meet your views—and a beautiful pictur' of Fumchoo on the cover, with the

Chinamen a-picking of the tea leaves. What! no bidder ? '

There ensued a pause. Every one expected that the girl would lower the price. They were mistaken. She went back into the van and produced a roll of calico. Then ensued an outcry of many voices: 'Tea! give us some of your tea, please.' In ten minutes she had disposed of all she had.

'There, you see,' said Zita, 'our supply runs short. In Wisbeach the Mayor and Corporation bought it, and at Cambridge all the colleges had their supplies from us. That's why we're run out now. Stand back, gents.'

This call was one of caution to the eager purchasers and tempted lookers-on.

Tawdry Fair was for horses and bullocks, and a drove of the latter was being sent along from the market-place towards Stuntney. For a while the business of the sale was interrupted. One audacious bullock even bounded into the

Galilee, another careered round the van; one
ran as if for sanctuary to the Bishop's palace.
Zita seized the occasion to slip inside the van.
Her father was on the low seat, leaning his
head wearily on his hand, and his elbow on his
knee.

'How are you now, dad?'

'I be bad, Zit—bad—tremenjous.'

'Had you not best see a doctor?'

He shook his head.

'It'll pass,' said he; 'I reckon doctors won't
do much for me. They're over much like us
Cheap Jacks—all talk and trash.'

'This has been coming on some time,'
observed the girl gravely. 'I've seen for a
fortnight you have been poorly.'

Then, looking forth between the curtains
which she had lowered, she saw that the
bullocks were gone, and that the cluster of
people interested in purchases had re-formed
round her little stage.

' I say,' shouted a chorister, ' have you got any pocket-knives ? '

' Pocket-knives by the score, and razors too. You'll be wanting a pair of them in a fortnight.'

Whilst Zita was engaged in furnishing the lads with knives, the Bishop retired from the upstairs window to his library, where he seated himself in an easy chair, took up a pamphlet and went up like a balloon inflated with elastic gas into theologic clouds, where controversy flashed and thundered about his head, and in this, his favourite sphere, the Right Reverend Father forgot all about the Cheap Jack, and no longer felt concern at his having been misrepresented as grovelling before a prince of the blood royal in a red waistcoat.

At the same time, also, a plot concerning Zita was being entered into by a number of young fenmen who had come to Tawdry Fair to amuse themselves, and had been arrested by the attractions of the Cheap Jack's van.

Whatever those attractions might have been whilst the man was salesman, they were enhanced tenfold when his place was occupied by his daughter. Some whispering had gone on for five minutes, and then with one consent they began to elbow their way forward till they had formed an innermost ring around the platform. But this centripetal movement had not been executed without difficulty and protest. Women, boys, burly men were forced to give way before the wedge-like thrusts inwards of the young men's shoulders, and they remonstrated, the women shrilly, the boys by shouts, the men with oaths and blows. But every sort of resistance was overcome, all remonstrances of whatever sort were disregarded, and Zita suddenly found herself surrounded by a circle of sturdy, tall fellows, looking up with faces expressive of mischief.

That something more than eagerness to purchase was at the bottom of this movement struck Zita, and for a moment she lost confidence, and faltered in her address on the excellence of some moth-eaten cloth she was endeavouring to sell.

Then one round-faced, apple-complexioned young man worked himself up by the wheel of the van, and, planting his elbows on the platform, shouted, 'Come, my lass, at what price do you sell kisses?'

'We ha'n't got them in the general stock,' answered Zita; 'but I'll ask father if he'll give you one.'

A burst of laughter.

'No, no,' shouted the red-faced youth, getting one knee on the stage. 'I'll pay you sixpence for a kiss—slick off your cherry lips.'

'I don't sell.'

'Then I'll have one as a gift.'

'I never give away nothing.'

'Then I'll steal one.'

The young fellow jumped to his feet on the

platform. At the signal the rest of the youths began to scramble up, and in a minute the place was invaded, occupied, and the girl surrounded. Cheers and roars of laughter rose from the spectators.

'Now, then, you Cheap Jack girl,' exclaimed the apple-faced youth. 'Kisses all round, three a-piece, or we'll play Old Harry with the shop, and help ourselves to its contents.'

The father of Zita, on hearing the uproar, the threats, the tramp of boots on the stage, staggered to his feet, and, drawing back the curtains, stood holding them apart, and looking forth with bewildered eyes. Zita turned and saw him.

'Sit down, father,' said she. 'It's only the general public on a frolic.'

She put her hand within and drew forth a stout ashen flail, whirled it about her head, and at once, like grasshoppers, the youths leaped from the stage, each fearing lest the flapper should fall on and cut open his own pate. The last to spring was the apple-faced youth; he was endeavouring to find some free space into which to descend, when the flapper of the flail came athwart his shoulder-blades with so sharp a stroke, that, uttering a howl, he plunged among the throng, and would have knocked down two or three, had they not been wedged together too closely to be upset.

Then ensued cries from those hurt by his weight as he floundered upon them; cries of 'Now, then, what do you mean by this? Can't you keep to yourself? This comes of your nonsense.'

Zita stood erect, leaning on the staff of the flail, looking calmly round on the confusion, waiting till the uproar ceased, that she might resume business. As she thus stood, her eye rested on a tall, well-shaped man, with a tiger's skin cast over his broad shoulders, and with a black felt slouched hat on his head. His nose was like the beak of a hawk. His eyes were dark, piercing, and singularly close together, under brows that met in one straight band across his forehead.

The moment this man's eye caught that of Zita, he raised his great hat, flourished it in the air, exposing a shaggy head with long dark locks, and he shouted, 'Well done, girl! I like that. Give me a pair of them there ashen flails, and here's a crown for your pluck.'

'I haven't a pair,' said the girl.

'Then I'll have that one, with which a little gal of sixteen has licked our Fen louts. I like that.'

'I'll give you a crown for that flail,' called another man, from the farther side of the crowd. 'Here you are—a crown.'

This man was fair, with light whiskers—a tall man as well as the other, and about the same age.

'I'll give you seven shillings and six — a

I.—3

crown and half a crown for that flail,' roared
the dark man. 'I bid first—I want that flail.'

'Two crowns — ten shillings,' called the fair
man. 'I can make a better offer than Drownlands—not as I want the flail, but as Drownlands wants it, he shan't have it.'

'Twelve and six,' roared the dark man.
'Gold's no object with me. What I wants I
will have.'

The lookers-on nudged each other. A young
farmer said to his fellow, 'Them chaps, Runham
and Drownlands, be like two tigers; when they
meet they must fight. We shall have fun.'

'You are a fool!' shouted the fair man,—'a
fool—that is what I think you are, to give
twelve and six for what isn't worth two shillings.
I'll let you have it at that price, that you may
become the laughing-stock of the Fens.'

The flail was handed out of the van to the
man called Drownlands, Zita received a piece
of gold and half a crown in her palm. She

retired into the waggon, and immediately re-appeared with a second flail.

'Here is another, after all,' said she; 'I didn't think I had it.'

'I'll take that to make the pair,' said Drown-lands; 'but as you've done me over the first, I think you should give me this one.'

'I done you?' exclaimed Zita; 'you've done yourself.'

'She's right there,' observed a man in the crowd. 'Them tigers — Runham and Drown-lands—would fight about a straw.'

'Are you going to hand me over that flail?' asked the dark purchaser.

Zita remained for a moment undecided. She had in verity made an unprecedented price with the first, and she was half inclined to surrender the second gratis, but to give and receive nothing was against the moral code of Cheap Jacks from the beginning of Cheap Jacking. Whilst she hesitated, holding the flail in suspense, and with a finger on her lips, the fair man yelled out—

'Don't let the blackguard have it. I'll have it to spoil the pair for him, and for no other reason.'

'I will have it, you scoundrel!' howled the dark man. 'I have as much gold as ever you have. I don't care what I spend. Here, girl! a crown to begin with.'

'Seven and six,' shouted Runham.

'Ten shillings,' cried Drownlands.

'Fifteen shillings!' exclaimed the fair man. Then, seeing that his rival was about to bid, he yelled, 'A guinea!' at the same moment that the other called, 'A pound!'

'It is yours,' said the girl to the man Runham, and she handed him the flail. She saw that the passions of the two men were roused, and she deemed it desirable to close the scene, lest a fight should ensue, in which, possibly, she might lose the money that had been offered.

Runham, flourishing his flail over his head, and throwing out the flapper in the direction of Drownlands, said, 'There, now! Who can say but what I'm the best off of the two? Mine cost me a guinea, and his beggarly flail not above twelve and six. I am the better man of the two by eight and six.'

He felt in his pockets and drew forth a guinea.

'There, you Cheap Jack girl—here's your money all in gold. I'm the better man of the two by eight and six. I've beat Drownlands like a gentleman.'

Some one looking on in the crowd said, 'A pair o' flails and a pair o' fools at the end o' them, as don't know what is the vally o' their money. Never since the creation of the world was flails sold at that price, and never will be again.'

'And never would have been, or never could have been, anywhere but among fen-tigers,' said another.

'I'll tell'y what,' observed the first; 'this ain't the end o' the story.'

'No—I guess not. It's the beginnin' rather of a mighty queer tale.'

CHAPTER III

TWO CROWNS

A STRANGELY interesting city is Ely. Unique in its way is the metropolis of the Fens; wonderful exceeding it must have been in the olden times when the fen-land was one great inland sea, studded at wide intervals with islets as satellites about the great central isle of Ely. It was a scene that impressed the imagination of our forefathers. Stately is the situation of Durham, that occupies a tongue of land between ravines. It has its own unique and royal splendour. But hardly if at all inferior, though very different, is the situation of Ely. The fens extend on all sides to the horizon, flat as the sea, and below the sea level. If the dykes were broken through, or the steam pumps and windmills ceased to work, all would again, in a twelvemonth, revert to its primitive condition of a vast inland sea, out of which would rise the marl island of Ely, covered with buildings amidst tufted trees, reflecting themselves in the still water as in a glass. Above the roofs, above the tree-tops, soars that glorious cathedral, one of the very noblest, certainly one of the most beautiful, in England—nay, let it be spoken boldly—in the whole Christian world. It stands as a beacon seen from all parts of the Fens, and it is the pride of the Fens.

Ely owes its origin to a woman—St. Etheldreda—flying from a rude, dissolute, and drunken court. She was the wife first of Tombert, a Saxon prince in East Anglia, then of Egfrid of Northumbria. Sick of the coarse revelry, the rude manners of a Saxon court, Etheldreda fled and hid herself in the isle of Ely, where she would be away from men and alone with God and wild, beautiful nature.

Whatever we may think of the morality of
a wife deserting her post at the side of her
husband, of a queen abandoning her position in
a kingdom, we cannot, perhaps, be surprised at
it. A tender, gentle-spirited woman after a
while sickened of the brutality of the ways of
a Saxon court, its drunkenness and savagery,
and fled that she might find in solitude that
rest for her weary soul and overstrained nerves
she could not find in the Northumbrian palace.
This was in the year 673. Then this islet
was unoccupied. It has been supposed that
it takes its name from the eels that abounded
round it; we are, perhaps, more correct in sur-
mising that it was originally called the Elf-isle,
the islet inhabited by the mythic spiritual
beings who danced in the moonlight and
sported over the waters of the meres.

This lovely island, covered with woods, surrounded by a fringe of water-lilies, gold and
silver, floating far out as a lace about it, became

the seat of a great monastery. Monks succeeded the elves.

King Canute, the Dane, was seized with admiration for Ely, loved to visit it in his barge, or come to it over the ice. It is said that one Candlemas Day, when, as was his wont, King Canute came towards Ely, he found the meres overflowed and frozen. A 'ceorl' named Brithmer led the way for Canute's sledge over the ice, proving the thickness of the ice by his own weight. For this service his lands were enfranchised.

On another occasion the king passed the isle in his barge, and over the still and glassy water came the strains of the singing in the minster. Whereupon the king composed a song, of which only the first stanza has been preserved, that may be modernised thus :—

> ' Merry sang the monks of Ely
> As King Knut came rowing by.
> Oarsmen, row the land more near
> That I may hear their song more clear.'

Ely, although it be a city, is yet but a village. The houses are few, seven thousand inhabitants is the population, it has two or three parish churches, and the cathedral, the longest in Christendom. The houses are of brick or of plaster; and a curious custom exists in Ely of encrusting the plaster with broken glass, so that a house-front sparkles in the sun as though frosted. All the roofs are tiled. The cathedral is constructed of stone quarried in Northamptonshire, and brought in barges to the isle.

Ely possesses no manufactures, has almost no neighbourhood, stands solitary and self-contained. On some sides it rises rapidly from the fen, on others it slopes easily down. A singular effect is produced when the white mists hang over the fen-land for miles and miles, and the sun glitters on the island city. Then it is as an enchanted isle of eternal spring, lost in a wilderness of level snow. Or again, on a night when the auroral lights flicker over the heavens, here red, there silvery, and against the glowing skies towers up this isle, crowned with its mighty cathedral, then, verily, it is as though it were a scene in some fairy tale, some magic creation of Eastern fantasy.

A girl was sauntering through the wide, grass-grown streets of Ely. During the fair the streets were full of people—nay, full is not the word—were occupied by people more or less scattered about them. It would take a vast throng, such as the fens of Cambridgeshire cannot supply, to *fill* these wide spaces.

The girl was tall and handsome, rather masculine, with a cheerful face. She had very fair hair, a bright complexion, and eyes of a dazzling blue—a blue as of the sea when rippling and sparkling in the midsummer sun. She was plainly dressed in serge of dark navy blue with white kerchief about her neck, a chip hat-bonnet, and blue ribbons in it. Her skirts were somewhat short, they exposed neat ankles in

stockings white as snow, and strong shoes. A
fen-girl must wear strong shoes, she cannot have
gloves on her feet.

'Jimminy!' said the girl, as she turned her
pocket inside out. 'Not one penny! Poor
Kainie is the only girl at the fair without a
sweetheart, the only child without a fairing.
No one to treat me! Nothing to be got for
nothing. Jimminy! I don't care.' Then she
began to sing :—

> ' Last night the dogs did bark,
>   I went to the gate to see,
> When every lass had her spark,
>   But nobody comes to me.
>   And it's Oh dear! what will become of me?
>   Oh dear, what shall I do?
>   Nobody coming to marry me,
>   Nobody coming to woo.
>
> My father's a hedger and ditcher,
>   My mother does nothing but spin,
> And I am a pretty young girl,
>   But the money comes slowly in '—

Then suddenly she confronted the fair-haired
farmer Runham, coming out of a tavern, with

the flail over his shoulder. A little disconcerted at encountering him, she paused in her song, but soon recovered herself, and began again at the interrupted verse :—

> ‘ My father's a hedger and ditcher,
> My mother ’—

‘ Kainie ! Are you beside yourself, singing like a ballad-monger in the open street ? ’

The man's face was red, whether with drink, or that the sight of the girl had brought the colour into his face, Kainie could not say. His breath smelt of spirits, and she turned her head away.

‘ It's all nonsense,’ she said. ‘ My mother is dead—is dead—and I am alone. I don't know, I don't see why I should not sing ; I want a fairing, and have no money. I'll go along singing, “ My father's a hedger and ditcher,” and then some charitable folk will throw me coppers, and I shall get a little money and buy myself a fairing.’

'For heaven's sake, do nothing of the kind. Here — rather than that — here is a crown. Take that. What would the Commissioners say if they were told that you went a ballad-singing in the streets of Ely at Tawdry Fair? They would turn you out of your mill. I am sure they would. Here, Kainie, conduct yourself respectably, and take a crown.'

He pressed the large silver coin into her hand, and hurried away.

'That's brave!' exclaimed the girl, snapping her fingers. 'Now I can buy my fairing. Now, all I want is a lover.

> " Nobody coming to marry me,
>   Nobody coming to woo."

Jimminy! I must not do that! I've taken a crown to be mum. Now I'm a young person of respectability—I've money in my pocket. Now I must look about me and see what to buy. I'll go to the Cheap Jack. How do you do, uncle?'

She addressed the dark-haired man Drown-lands, who had just turned the corner, with his flail over his shoulder. He scowled at the girl, and would have passed her without a word, but to this she would not consent.

'See! see!' said she, holding up the crown she had received. 'I was just going along sighing and weeping because I had no money, not a farthing in my pocket, not a lover at my side to buy me anything. Then came some one and gave me this—look, Uncle Drownlands! Five shillings!'

'So—going in bad ways?'

'What is the harm? I was ballad-singing. Then he came and gave me a crown.'

'You ballad-singing?'

'Yes; how else can I get money? I'm a poor girl, owned by nobody, for whom nobody cares.'

'You will bring disgrace—deeper disgrace on the family—on the name.'

'Not I; I'm honest. If I am given five

shillings, may I not receive it? Master Runham gave me the money to make me shut my
mouth. I was singing

> "My father's a hedger and ditcher,
>   My mother"'—

'For heaven's sake, silence!' said Drownlands
angrily. 'If you will hold your tongue, I will
give you a couple of shillings.'

'A couple of shillings? And I'm your own
niece, and have your name!'

'More shame to you—to your mother!' exclaimed the farmer bitterly.

The girl suddenly dropped her head, and her
brow became crimson.

'Not a word about my dear mother—not a
stone thrown at her,' she said in a low tone.

'Well, no ballad-singing. Take heed to yourself. You are wild and careless.'

'Much you think of me! much you care for
me!'

'Begone! You are a disgrace to me—your

existence is a disgrace. Take a crown and spend it properly. You shall have nothing more from me. As Runham gave you five shillings, it shall not be said that I gave you less.'

He handed her the coin, and with a scowl passed on.

Kainie remained for a moment musing, with lowered eyes. Then she raised her head, shook it, as though to shake off the sadness, the humiliation that had come on her with the words of Drownlands, and hummed—

> ' Nobody coming to marry me,
> Nobody coming to woo.'

' What ! Kainie ! '

The words were those of a young man, heavy-browed, pale, somewhat gaunt, with long arms.

' Oh, Pip !—Pip !—Pip ! '

' What is the matter, Kainie ? '

' Pip, I'm the only girl here without her

young man. It is terrible—terrible; and see,
Pip, I've got two crowns to spend, and I don't
know what to spend them on. There is too
much money here for sweetie stuff; and as for
smart ribbons and bonnets and such like, it is
only just about once in the year I can get away
from the mill and come into town and show
myself. It does seem a waste to spend a couple
of crowns on dress, when no one can see me
rigged out in it. What shall I do, Pip?—you
wise, you sensible, you dear Pip.'

The young man, Ephraim Beamish, considered; then he said—

'Kainie, I don't like your being alone in Red
Wings. Times are queer. Times will be worse.
There is trouble before us in the Fens. Things
cannot go on as they are—the labouring men
ground down under the heels of the farmers,
who are thriving and waxing fat. I don't like
you to be alone in the windmill; you should
have some protector. Now, look here. I've

been to that Cheap Jack van, and there's a big dog there the Cheap Jackies want to sell, but there has been no bid. Take my advice, offer the two crowns for that great dog, and take him home with you. Then I shall be easy ; and now I am not that. You are too lonely—and a good-looking girl like you '—

' Pip, I'll have the dog.' She tossed the coins into the air. ' Here, crownies, you go for a bow-wow.'

CHAPTER IV

ON THE DROVE

THERE is not in all England—there is hardly in the world—any tract of country more depressing to the spirits, more void of elements of loveliness, than the Cambridgeshire Fens as they now are.

In former days, when they were under water —a haunt of wildfowl, a wilderness of lagoons, a paradise of wild-flowers—when they teemed with fish and swarmed with insect life of every kind—when the *eys* or islets, Stuntney, Shipey, Southeoney, Welney, were the sole objects that broke the horizon, rising out of the marshes, rich with forest-trees—then the Fens were full of charm, because given over to Nature. But the industry of man has changed the character and aspect of the Fens. The meres have been pumped dry, the bogland has been drained. Where the fowler used to boat after wild duck, now turnips are hoed ; where the net was drawn by the fisherman, there wave cornfields.

In former times, for five-and-twenty miles north of Ely, one rippling lake extended, and men went by boat over it to the sand-dune that divided it from the sea at King's Lynn. To the west a mighty mere stretched from Ely to Peterborough. To the east lay a tangle of lake and channel, of marsh and islet.

Until about a hundred years ago, men lived in houses erected on platforms sustained upon piles above the level of the water. Walls and roofs of these habitations were thatched and wattled with reeds. From the door a ladder conducted to a boat. In these houses there were hearths, but no chimneys. The smoke escaped as best it might through the thatch, or under the gables.

During the winter the fen-men picked up a livelihood fishing and fowling. In summer they cultivated such patches of peat soil as appeared above the surface of the water. There were no roads; men went from place to place by water, in boats or on skates.

In the reign of James I. Ben Jonson wrote his play 'The Devil is an Ass.' Into this play he introduced a speculator—a starter of bogus companies, by name Meercraft, and one of this man's schemes was the draining of the Fens.

'The thing is for recovery of drown'd land,
Whereof the Crown's to have a moiety,
If it be owner; else the Crown and owners
To share that moiety, and the recoverers
To enjoy the t'other moiety for their charge,
.   .   .   .   .   . which will arise
To eighteen millions, seven the first year.
I have computed all, and made my survey
Unto an acre; I'll begin at the pan,
Not at the skirts, as some have done, and lost
All that they wrought, their timberwork, their trench,
Their banks, all borne away, or else filled up
By the next winter. Tut! they never went
The (right) way. I'll have it all.

> A gallant tract of land it is ;
> 'Twill yield a pound an acre ;
> We must let cheap ever at first.'

Jonson introduced this Meercraft as a caution to the people of his day against being induced to sink money in such ventures, which he regarded as impossible of realisation. Nevertheless, what Jonson disbelieved in has been accomplished. The work begun in 1630, was interrupted by the Civil Wars, resumed afterwards, was carried on at considerable outlay and with great perseverance, till at the beginning of the present century the complete recovery of the Fens was an accomplished fact.

Great was the cost of the undertaking, and those who had invested in it wearied of the calls on their purses; land, or rather water, owners were discouraged, and were ready to part with rights and possessions that hardly fetched a shilling an acre, and which instead of

being drained itself seemed to be draining their
pockets. Long-headed fen-men saw their advantage, and bought eagerly where the owners
sold eagerly. The new canals carried off the
water, the machines set in operation discharged
the drainage into the main conduits, and soil
that for centuries had been worthless became
auriferous. No more magnificent corn-growing
land was to be found in England. None in
Europe might compare with it, save the delta of
the Danube and the richest alluvial tracts in
South Russia. The fen-men made their fortunes
before they had learned what to do with the
fortunes they made. Money came faster than
they found means to spend it.

To this day many of the wealthiest owners
are sons or grandsons of half-wild fen-slodgers.
There are no villages in the Fens apart from
such as are clustered on widely dispersed islets.
There are no old picturesque farmhouses and
cottages. Everything is new and ugly. There

are no hedges, no walls, for there is no stone in the country. There are no trees, save a few willows and an occasional ash, from whose roots the soil has shrunk. The surface of the land is sinking. As the fen is drained, the spongy soil contracts, and sinks at the rate of two inches in the year. Consequently houses built on piles are left after fifty years some eight feet above the surface, and steps have to be added to enable the inmates to descend from their doors.

The rivers slide along on a level with the top storeys of the houses, and the only objects to break the horizon are the windmills that drive the water up from the dykes into the canals.

There are no roads, as there is no material of which roads can be made. In place of roads there are 'droves.' A drove is a broad course, straight as an arrow, by means of which communication is had between one farm and

another, and people pass from one village to
another.

These droves have ditches, one on each side,
dense in summer with bulrushes. No attempt
is made to consolidate the soil in these droves
other than by harrowing and rolling them in
summer. In winter they are bogs, in summer
they are dust—dust black, impalpable. Wheeled
conveyances can hardly get along the droves in
winter, or wet weather, as the wheels sink to
the axles.

The canal banks, however, are solid, com-
pacted of stiff clay, and as they are broad, so as
to resist the pressure of the water they contain
between them, their tops make very tolerable
paths, and roads for those on horseback. But
no wheeled vehicle is suffered to use the bank
tops, and to prevent these banks from being
converted into carriage roads, barriers are placed
across them at intervals, which horses with
riders easily leap.

At one of the Cambridge Assizes a poor man, a witness in court, when asked his profession, answered,—'My lord, I am a banker.' The judge, turning very red, said, 'No joking here, sir.' 'But I *am* a banker and nothing else,' protested the witness. He was, in fact, one of the gang of men maintained for the reparation of the canal banks.

The reader must be given some idea of the manner in which this vast level region is drained. It is cut up into large squares, and each square is a field that is surrounded by dykes. These dykes are in communication with one another, and all lead to a *drain* or *load*, that is to say, to a channel of water of a secondary size, that lies at the level of a few feet above the dykes. To convey the water from the ditches into the drains, windmills are erected, that work machinery which throws the water out of the ditches up hill into the loads. These loads or drains run to the canal at intervals of two miles, and when the drain reaches the canal bank, then a pump of great power forces the water of the load to a still higher level, into the main artery through which it flows to the sea. On the canals are lighters, and these, rather than waggons, serve for the conveyance of farm produce to the markets. Water is the natural highway in the fen-land.

The short October day had closed in. The fen lay black, streaked with steely bands—the dykes that reflected the grey sky.

On the right hand was a bank rising some fourteen feet above the roadway; it was the embankment of the river or canal that goes by the name of the Lark, Above it, some wan stars were flickering. On the left hand the fen stretched away into infinity, the horizon was lost in fog.

The Cheap Jack's horse was crawling, reeling along the drove under the embankment, the van plunging into quagmires, lurching into ruts.

The horse strained every muscle and drew it forward a few yards, then sighed, hung his head, and remained immovable. Once again he nerved himself to the effort, and as the van started, its contents tinkled and rattled. The brute might as well have been drawing it across a ploughed field. Again he heaved a heavy sigh, and then finally abandoned the effort.

The Cheap Jack had got out of the conveyance. He was unwell, too unwell to walk, but he could not think of adding his weight to that the poor horse was compelled to drag over what was not the apology for, but the mockery of a road.

'I say, Zit,' muttered he hoarsely, 'I wish now as we'd a' stayed overnight in Ely.'

'I wish we had, father. And we could have afforded it; we've made fine profits in Ely— tremenjous.'

The man did not respond. He trudged and stumbled on.

The drove was as intolerable to walk on as to drive along.

'Well, I never came along roads like these afore,' said the girl, 'and I hopes we may soon be out of the Fens, and never get into them again.'

'I don't know as we shall ever get out,' said the man, reeling as one drunk. 'It seems as if we was sinking—sinking—and the black mud would close over us.'

'Come along, Jewel!' said Zita to the old horse. 'I'd put the lash of the whip across you, but I haven't the heart to do it.'

'This is going like snails,' groaned the man.

'It's going worse than snails,' retorted his daughter. 'Snails carry their houses safely along with them, but I doubt if we shall convey our van out of this here region o' stick-in-the-mud, without all it's in'ards being knocked to bits. We'll have to yarn tremenjous, father, to cover the dints in the tin and the cracks in the crocks.'

The man halted.

'I don't think I can get no forrarder,' said he ; 'I'm all of a quake and a chill.'

'Well, father, let us put up here. It's no odds to us where we stay.'

'But it is to the hoss. What's Jewel to eat? There's nought but mud and rushes. If we do take him out of the shafts, he'll tumble into one of the ditches.'

'I wonder what is the distance to Littleport?' asked the girl. 'But, bless me! on these roads it's no calculating distances. There was a man rode by us on the bank above. He had lanterns to his stirrups. I wish I'd gone up the side and just asked him how far ahead it was to Littleport. Now he's got a long way ahead, and it's no use to run after him.'

'We must go on. I doubt but we shall sink in the mire if we stay.'

The man sighed and staggered forward.
Then the horse also sighed and endeavoured to
move the van, but failed. It was fast.

'What is to be done now? There's Jewel
can't stir the caravan. Did you notice, father,
how that man's horse jumped as he rode by?
There is a sort of a rail across, or we would
have tried to get the conveyance up on the
bank. When the horse jumped, up went the
lanterns also. I suppose there is some farm
near here where they'll let us put up Jewel for
the night. We needn't trouble then, as we have
our own house on wheels. But Jewel must
have his food and a stall.'

At that moment a second rider appeared on
the embankment, trotting in the same direction
as had the first. He had a single lantern
attached to one stirrup, whereas the first who
had passed, and been noticed by Zita, had
two. The girl ran up the slope of the bank,
calling.

I.—5

The rider drew rein. 'What do you want?' he inquired.

'Oh, will you tell me where we can put our horse for the night and have a little hay?'

'Who are you?'

Zita knew by the tone of the voice that the man had been drinking, and that, though not inebriated, he had taken too much liquor—

'We are the Cheap Jack and his daughter. We cannot get along the way, it is so bad— and the wheels are stuck in the mud. We want to go to Littleport, and father'—

'You are a set of darned rascals!' interrupted the rider. 'I'll have nothing more to do with you; and you, I suppose, are the gal as cheated me—the worst of the lot you are.' He had a flail in his hand, and he flourished it over his head. 'You get along, you Cheap Jackies, or I'll bring the flail down about your heads and shoulders and loins, and make you fish out that there guinea I paid—and more fool I.' Driving his heels into the flanks of his horse, and slashing its neck with the loop of his bridle, he galloped along the top of the embankment.

Zita descended.

The van was stationary. The horse, Jewel, stood with drooping head and a pout on the nether lip, with legs stiff in the deep mire, resolute not to budge another inch. Zita took the van lantern and went to his head. Jewel had thrown an expression into his face that proclaimed his resolution not to make another effort, whether urged on by whip, or cajoled by caresses. The girl, still carrying the lantern, came to her father. He was seated against the embankment, with his hands in his pockets and his head fallen forward.

'Father, how are you?'

'Bad—bad—tremenjous.'

'Father, let us walk on and seek a house. Jewel will not stir; he has turned up his nose and set back his ears, and I know what that means. I don't think any one will come this way and rob the van. Let us go on together. You lean on me, and we will find a farm.'

'I can't rise, Zit.'

'Let me help you up.'

'I couldn't take another step, Zit.'

'Make an effort, father.'

'I'm past that, Zit. I'm dying. It's o' no use urging of me. I sticks here as does Jewel. I can't move. I'm too bad for that. O Lord! that I should die in this here fen-land!'

'Let me get you some brandy.'

'It ain't of no use at all, Zit. I'm just about done for. 'Tis so with goods at times; when they gets battered and bulged and broken and all to pieces, they must be chucked aside. I'm no good no more as a Cheap Jack. I'm battered and bulged and broken and all to pieces, so I'm going to be chucked aside.'

Zita considered for a moment. Then she set down the lantern at her father's side, ran up the embankment, ran along it in the direction which had been taken by the riders, one after the other, crying as loud as she possibly could, 'Help! help! Father is dying. Help! help! help!'

CHAPTER V

THE FLAILS AGAIN

HEZEKIAH, or, as he was usually called for short, Ki, Drownlands was riding homewards from the Ely Fair along the embankment of the river Lark. He bore over his shoulder the flail that had cost him twelve shillings and sixpence, and in his heart glowed a consuming rage that his adversary and neighbour—perhaps adversary because neighbour—Jeremiah or Jake Runham had paid a guinea for the companion flail, and had outbidden him.

It was not that Ki Drownlands particularly required a flail, or a companion flail to that he had secured, but he was intolerant of opposition, and it was his ambition to be first in his fen ; he

would show his supremacy by outbidding the
only man approaching him in wealth and in
influence, and that before a crowd made up in
part of people who knew him and his rival. It
was gall to his liver to think that he had been
surpassed in his offer, that an advantage over
him had been snatched, and that Jake Runham
had been able to carry off from under his nose
something—it muttered not what—that he, Ki
Drownlands, had coveted, and had let people
see that he had coveted.

The rivalry of these two landowners was
known throughout the Ely Fens, and in every
tavern the talk was certain to turn on the bidding
for the flails, and folk would say, ' Jake is a
better man than Ki by eight shillings and
sixpence.'

Drownlands had been drinking, and this fact
served to sharpen and inflame his resentment,
but he was able to ride upright and steadily,
and sit his horse upright and steadily as the

beast leaped the barriers on the bank. He
carried, as already mentioned, lanterns below
both feet attached to the stirrups. They
illumined the way, they flashed upon obstructions, they sent a gleam over the water of the
canal. In the dark—and the night was at times
pitch-dark, when clouds cut off the light of the
stars—then it was not safe to ride on the embankment without a light. The horse might
fail to see the barriers, and precipitate itself
against them. It might slip down the bank
and fall with its rider, on one side into the river,
on the other into the drove. On the one side
the horseman might be drowned, on the other
break his neck. But, supposing the horse had
its wits about it and its eyes open, the rider
might have neither, and be unprepared for the
leap, or the slip in the greasy marl.

If, conscious of the risk when on the embank-
men, the horseman took the drove; then also
he was not safe, for there it was doubly dark,

shadowed on one side by the elevation of the embankment, whilst on the other side lay the dyke, the water brimming, and disguised by sedge and rushes. Into this a horse might plunge, and, once in, could not be extricated without infinite labour by several hands. For the bottom of the ditches is soft bog, and the sides are spongy peat. Not a particle of firm substance can be found on which a horse may plant its feet, and obtain the purchase necessary for lifting itself out of the water and mire. Consequently, when farmers returned late from market and fair in the long dark winter nights, they provided themselves with lanterns.

Prickwillow was the name of the farm of Master Ki Drownlands. The grandfather of Ki had possessed a reed-walled cottage on piles, and a few acres of soil that showed above the water in March, was submerged again for a while in July, and then reappeared as the rainy season ceased. Here he was wont to prick in willow twigs that rapidly grew into osier beds. On a platform above the rippling water the grandfather had mended his nets and cleaned his fowling-piece, and the grandmother had woven baskets. Now all was dry, and a house stood where had been the lacustrine habitation, and the plough turned up the thousand odds and ends that successive generations had cast out of the cottage into the water, never expecting that they would be seen again.

The flood had retreated, dry land had appeared, and the ark had rested on what had formerly been the least submerged portion of the tract over which the ancestral slodger, Drownlands, had exercised more or less questionable rights ; rights, however, which, though questionable, had never been questioned. With a little money collected by industry, and more borrowed from the Ely bank, the *père* Drownlands had extended his domain, and had rendered his claim absolute and his rights unassailable.

And now Ki Drownlands was riding home in a fume of wounded pride, and with a brain somewhat turned by brandy. He sharply drew rein ; he thought he heard a cry. The cry was repeated as he halted to listen. From whence it came he could not judge, saving only that it proceeded from the rear. Over the fen, as upon water, sound travels great distances ; over the fen, as over water, meeting with no obstructions, the waves of sound pass, and it is not easy to judge distances. Drownlands turned his horse about and faced in the direction of Ely, the direction whence the call came, as far as he could judge.

He saw a light approaching. Was it carried, or hung to a stirrup? He could not tell. Was it the lantern-bearer who summoned him? If so, for what object? The cry was repeated.

Surely the voice was that of a female. If the appeal were not to him, to whom could it be addressed?

To the best of his knowledge, there was no one else out so late on the embankment. He recalled passing no one.

It was true that he had ridden by the van, but he had not seen it. The van was in the drove below, and he had been twelve or fourteen feet above the roadway. Moreover, the lanterns at his feet threw a halo about him, and though they illumined every object that came within their radius, yet they made all doubly obscure and everything indistinguishable that was outside that radius.

Furthermore, Drownlands had been occupied with his own thoughts, and had not been in an observant mood.

Zita had not addressed him as he rode by, and he had passed without any notion that there were travellers toiling along in the same direction at a lower level. He had not expected to see a conveyance there, and had looked for none.

The light that he noticed on the bank was

approaching. It was held at no great distance from the ground. It might equally be carried in the hand of one on foot, or be swung from the stirrups of a rider. It was, however, improbable that a horseman would be contented with a single light.

Drownlands did not ride forward to meet the advancing light. He remained stationary, with his right hand holding the flail, so that the end of the staff rested on his thigh, much as a field-marshal is represented in pictures holding his *baton*.

In the Fens the horses are unshod, and on a way that is without stones there will be little sound of a horse when trotting; but as the moving light neared, Drownlands was aware from the vibration of the embankment that a horse was approaching.

A minute later, and he saw before him Jake Runham, mounted.

The recognition was mutual.

'Out of my way!' shouted Runham. 'Out of my way, you dog, or I will ride you down!'

'I will not get out of your way. Why did you call?'

'I call? I call you? That's a likely tale. What should I want with a twopenny-ha'penny chap such as you?'

'Twopenny-ha'penny? Do you mean me?'

'Yes, I do.'

'You are drunk. Some one called.'

'Not I. But I call now, and loud enough. Stand out of my way; get down the side of the bank; and go to the devil.'

'I will not make way for you,' said Drownlands. Then between his teeth, 'It is well we have met.'

'Ay, it is well.'

'Now we can settle old scores. Now'—he looked up, and waved his flail towards heaven, which was clad with clouds —'now that no eyes look down from above, and we are quite sure there are no eyes watching us from below '—

Then Runham, with a yell, dug his spurs into the flanks of his steed, and made him bound forward. His intention was, with the impetus, to drive his adversary and horse down the bank. As it was, his horse struck that of Drownlands, which, being a heavy beast, swerved but slightly.

' Keep off, you drunken fool!' shouted Ki.

' Am I to keep off you? I? Not I. I will have the bank to myself. Let me pass, or I will ride over you and tread your brains out.'

' You will have the matter of the past fought out between us?'

'Ay! Ay!'

Jake backed his horse, snorting and plunging under the curb.

Then, when he had retired some twenty yards, he uttered a halloo, whirled his flail above his head, drove his heels into the sides of his steed, and came on at a gallop.

Drownlands raised and brandished his flail, and brought it down with a sweep before him. This alarmed his own horse, which reared and started, but more so that of his rival, which suddenly leaped on one side, and nearly unseated Jake Runham. However, Jake gripped the pommel, and with an oath urged his horse into the path again.

Drownlands had forgotten about the call that had induced him to turn his horse. His attention was solely occupied with the man before him.

The situation was one in which two resolute men, each determined not to yield to the other, each inflamed with anger against the other, must fight their controversy out to the end. The way on the bank top would not admit of two abreast, consequently not of one passing the other without mutual concession. On the one side was the drove fourteen feet below, on the other the canal. He who had to give way

must roll down the embankment into the drove
or plunge into the water.

Each man was armed, and each with a like
weapon.

It would seem as though the horses understood
the feelings that actuated their riders, and shared
them. They snorted defiance, they tossed their
manes, they reared and pawed the air.

Again Runham spurred his steed, and the
beasts clashed together, and as they did so, so
also did the flails.

The two men were at close quarters, too
close for the flappers of the flails to take full
effect. They heaved their weapons and struck
furiously at each other, bruising flesh, but
breaking no bones. The strokes of the whistling flappers fell on the saddle back, on the sides
of the horses, rather than on the heads and
shoulders of the men. The lanterns jerked
and danced, as the horses pawed and plunged,
and bit at each other.

The men swore, and strove by main weight to force each other from the bank,—Runham to drive his antagonist into the river, Drownlands by side blows of the flail to force the opposed horse to go down the bank into the drove.

The struggle lasted for some minutes. To any one standing by it would have seemed a confusion of dancing lights and reflections—a confusion also of oaths, blows, and clash of steel bits, and thud of ashen staves.

Then, by mutual consent, but unexpressed, the two men drew back equally exhausted. They drew back with no thought of yielding, but with intent to recover wind and strength to renew the contest. Both antagonists remained planted opposite each other, panting, quivering with excitement, their beasts steaming in the cold October night air.

'You dared to call me by an ugly name before folk!' shouted Drownlands.

'Dared ? —I will do it again.'

'You shall not be given the chance.'

'I carried away the flail over your head because you hadn't more shillings in your pocket.'

'The flail?' echoed Drownlands. 'This is
not a matter now of a flail. This is not a
matter now of a way along the bank. It's a
matter of nineteen years' endurance. For
nineteen years I have borne the grossest of
wrongs. I'll bear the burden no longer. The
wrong shall not go another hour unavenged.'

'You've borne it so long the back is accustomed to the burden,' taunted Jake.

'For nineteen years I have endured it. But
to-night we are face to face, and alone.' Again
he waved his flail to heaven. 'No eye looks
down upon us. I and you are equally matched
as far as weapons go. All is fair between us,
but if there be justice on high, it will weight
my arm to beat you down; and here,' said he,
touching his breast with the end of the flail,—
'here is no spark of pity, just as there is now

no spark aloft. If I beat you, I beat you till the blood runs, beat you till the bones are pounded, beat you till the marrow oozes out, beat you—as we beat hemp.'

Then, unable longer to control his fury, the dark man urged his horse forward with his spurs, and as he did so the lanterns clashed against the flanks of the brute, and burnt them as the spurs had stung them. With a snort of anger and pain, the beast leaped into the air, flung himself forward, and hurled his whole weight against the horse of Runham. The latter had altered his tactics, and had drawn up to receive the charge instead of delivering it as before. At the same moment Ki swung his flail and brought it down. But he had over-shot his mark, and with the violence of the blow he was carried across the neck of Runham's horse. Jake saw his advantage at once, caught him by the tiger-skin, and, grappling that, endeavoured to drag his opponent out of the saddle. But Ki reared himself up, and tried to wrench the skin away. His bodily strength was the greatest. The horses leaped, kicked, reeled, and the two men on them held fast, the tiger-skin between them. Then Runham twisted his flail in the skin and continued to turn it. In vain now did Ki endeavour to wrench it away. The skin was fast about his throat, and as it was drawn tighter and even tighter, it threatened strangulation. Jake backed his horse, and as he backed, he drew his opponent after him. The blood thumped in the ears of Drownlands. The veins in his temples swelled to bursting.

The plunging of the horses caused the pressure to be relaxed for one moment, but it was tightened the next, and became intolerable. Ki's tongue and eyes started, his lips were puffed, foam formed on them. He could not cry, he could not speak, he snuffled and gasped. With his heels he thrust his horse forward, to save himself from being drawn from his saddle to hang to the flail of Runham.

In another moment Drownlands would have been unhorsed and at his adversary's mercy. But at this supreme instant he clutched his own flail, and, holding it with both hands over his bent head, drove the end of it into the ear of Runham's horse. The more he was drawn forward, the greater the leverage on the end of his flail, and the more exquisite the agony of the horse. The brute, driven mad with pain, gathered itself up into a convulsive, spasmodic shake and leap, and with the jerk, the tiger-skin was plucked out of the hand of Jake Runham.

Drownlands reared himself in his stirrups. He was blinded with blood in his eyes, but he whirled the flail round his head, and beat savagely in all directions. It whistled as it swung, it screamed as it descended. Then a thud, a cry, and indistinctly, through the roar of his pulses in his ears, he heard a crash down the bank, and indistinctly through his suffused eyes he saw a black mass stagger into the river.

Gasping for breath, quivering in every nerve, tingling in every vein, as the blood recovered its wonted circulation, Drownlands held his horse motionless, and, gathering his senses, looked before him.

There was hardly a flake of steely light in the sky. Clouds had spread over the firmament. What little light there was, lay as a strip on the horizon, like the glaze of white in a dead man's eye. The inky water reflected none of it. For a moment, on the surface, the lantern attached to Runham's stirrup floated and danced, whilst the flame burnt and charred the horn side, then it was drawn under and extinguished.

Drownlands leaned forward and stretched his flail to the water; then drew the flapper across the surface where his enemy had sunk, as one who scratches out a score.

Then suddenly he was grasped by the foot, and a voice rang in his ears : 'Help! help! Oh, prithee, help!'

In his condition of nervous excitation, the touch, the call, so unexpected, wrung from him a scream. It was as though a rude hand had fallen on an exposed nerve.

Again a tighter clasp at his foot, again an entreating cry of intenser entreaty : 'Help! Oh, prithee, prithee, help!'

CHAPTER VI

BETWEEN TWO LIGHTS

ZITA had run on. Her young heart was full of the agony of distress for her father. He was the one object in the world to whom her heart clung. She had lost her mother early, and had been accordingly brought up by her father, who had been father and mother to her in one. She had no brothers, no sisters. He had been to her father, mother, brothers, and sisters in one. The young heart is full of love. It is of a clinging nature. It may not be disposed to demonstrativeness, but it loves, it clings; and it is in despair when the object to which it has clung, the person it has loved, fails.

89

For some little while, for more than the fortnight of which Zita had spoken, she had observed that her father was ill, that his powers were declining.

She had fought against the terrible thought that she would lose him, whenever with a flash of horror it had shot through her brain, had contracted her heart.

Her father! The daily associate; the one person to whom she could always speak with frankness, with whom she had had but one interest; the one person who had watched over her, cared for her, loved her—that he should be suffering, that he might be removed! The idea was more than her young heart could bear. Cheap Jacks are human beings, they have like feelings to us who buy not of Cheap Jacks, but of respectable tradesmen. Cheap Jacks' daughters, though they have not had the privileges of the moral and intellectual training that have ours, are nevertheless—human beings. We admit this tacitly, but do not think out the truth such an admission contains—that they have in their natures the same mixed propensities, in their hearts the same passions as ourselves—as have our own children.

Now this poor child ran, her pulses beating ; as she ran, with every rush of blood through her pulses, a fire shot in electric flashes before her eyes. She continuously cried, 'Help! help! My father! my daddy!'

Then her breath failed her. She tried to run, but was forced to stay her feet and gasp for breath. She could not maintain her pace as well as call for assistance.

There was a roaring as of the sea over a bar when the tide is coming in. It was the roar of her thundering blood in her ears.

She had taken the van lantern and had set it down by her father on the side of the bank. As she was forced to halt, she looked back. A shudder came over her. She could not see the light. Had it expired, and with it, had the flickering light of life expired in her father?

Then she stepped partly down the bank, and now she saw the light. From the top she had not been able to see it owing to the slope, and for a slight curve in the direction of the canal. The light that burned by her father's side was still there. And before her she could see the sparks in the direction she was pursuing. A strange medley of lights—were there two or three or more? She could not count, owing to her excitement and the tears and sweat that streamed over her eyes.

She ran on, as the furious throbbing of her heart was allayed, as her breath returned.

Suddenly—a crash, a flash as of lightning, and Zita knew not where she was, and for how long she had been in a state of semi-consciousness.

The poor child, running with full speed, had run against one of the barriers set up across the top of the embankment for the prevention of its employment by wheeled vehicles.

She had struck her head and chest against the bars, and had been thrown backwards, partly stunned, completely dazzled by the blow. For some minutes she lay on the bank confused and in pain. Then she picked herself up, but was unable to understand what had happened. She again went forward, and now felt the bars of timber. She put her hands to them and climbed. She was sobbing with pain and anxiety; through her tears she could see the lights in front of her magnified with prismatic rays shooting from them. On reaching the top of the barrier she looked behind her, and again saw the feeble light from her father's lantern.

Now her senses returned to her, which for a few moments had been disturbed by the blow and fall.

She was running to obtain help, shelter for her dear father. From the top rail she cried,

'Help! help! My daddy! My poor daddy! Help! help!'

She listened. She thought she heard voices. Hurt, wearied, breathless, she hoped that the assistance she had invoked was coming to her aid.

Should she remain perched where she was, and wait till the lights in front drew nearer to her?

Then the fear came over her that she might not have been heard. The man to whom she had spoken—he with the one lantern to his stirrup—had addressed her roughly, had shown no good feeling, no desire to assist. Was it likely that he had changed his mind, and was now returning?

She was confident that the man whom she had arrested had carried but a single lantern to his foot. Now as her pulses became more even in their throb, she was positive that there were more lights than one before her. She looked

behind her.   There was one light by her father;
that was stationary.   There were several before
her; and they were in the strangest movement,
flickering here and there, changing places, now
obscured, now shining out, now low, now high,
now on this side, now on that.

She leaped from her place on the rail and
ran on.

Then, coming on an unctuous place in the
marl, where a horse's hoofs had been, where,
perhaps, it had slipped, and, running in a bee-
line, regardless where she went, ignorant of a
slight deviation from the direct line in the
course of the bank, she went down the side, and
plunged into the ice-cold water.

There was a stake, a post in the water.   She
clung to that, and, holding it, struggled to get
out.   In so doing, she noticed a sort of eye in
the post, a mortice-hole that pierced it, and as
at that moment some of the clouds had parted,
she saw the grey sky and a star shine through

this hole. By means of this post, Zita, whose strength was almost spent, was able to draw herself from out of the water. But so exhausted was she, that, on reaching the top of the bank, she was constrained to stop and pant for breath.

Still the thought of her suffering, perhaps dying, father, urged her on. She saw the dancing lights close before her, she heard voices. She felt the embankment tremble under her feet. Surely some violent commotion was taking place before her; but what it could be she had neither time nor power to conjecture.

Then there went by overhead, invisible in the darkness, a train of wild geese, going south for the winter, and as they flew they uttered loud, wild cries, like the barking of hounds in the clouds—a horrible, startling sound fit to unnerve any who were unaware of the cause.

For a moment she stood still, listening to the aerial ghostly sounds. She held her breath. Then again she ran.

As Zita ran, it seemed to her that assuredly she saw but two lights. There must have been but two, and they were stationary. She tried to call, but her voice failed her ; her throat was parched. She could but run.

Next moment the lights blazed large on her, and then she grasped a foot. 'Help! help!'

CHAPTER VII

PROFITS

'WHAT do you want? Who are you?' asked Ki Drownlands, when he had sufficiently recovered his self-possession to see that some one was clinging to him, and that that person was a woman.

'Help! Come back! Father is ill.'

'I don't care. Let go. You hurt me.'

She hurt him by her touch on his boot! His nerves were thrilling, and the pressure of her fingers was unendurable in the surexcitation of every fibre of his system.

'Oh, help! help!' She would not relax her hold.

'I cannot. I've my own concerns to attend.'

Drownlands remained silent for a moment.
He was shivering as one in an ague fit—shivering as though the marrow in his bones were
touched with frost. Presently he asked in a
voice of constraint—

'How long have you been here? What have
you seen?'

He stooped to his stirrup, unhitched one of
the lanterns and held it aloft, above the person
who appealed for his aid.

The dim yellow light fell over a head of
thick amber hair and a pale, beautifully moulded
face, with large lustrous eyes, looking up en-
treatingly at him.

His hand that held the lantern was unsteady,
and the light quivered. To disguise his agita-
tion, he gave the lantern a pendulous motion, and
the reflection glinted and went out, glinted again
in those great beseeching eyes, and glowed in that
copper-gold hair, as though waves of glory flashed
up in the darkness and set again in darkness.

'What have you seen?' he repeated.

'Seen?—I see you. I want help. You will help me?'

'How long have you been here?'

'How long? I am but this instant come. I have run.'

Her bosom was heaving under a gay kerchief, her breath came in little puffs of steam that passed as golden dust in the halo of the lantern.

Drownlands rested both his hands on the pommel of the saddle, with the flail athwart beneath them. He put the handle of the lantern in his mouth, and the upward glare of the light was on his sinister face. He was considering. He did not recognise the girl. His mind was too distraught to think whether or not he had seen her before. She persisted.

'Help us! I have been running. I am out of breath. I saw you ride by on the bank. I called to you, and spoke to you there, and you would do nothing. My dear father is worse. He is dying. You must—you shall help.'

He still looked at her. That beautiful face— the sole object shining out of the darkness— fascinated him, in spite of his alarm, his distress.

'I am Cheap Jack Zita. I am the daughter of the poor Cheap Jack. He is taken ill—he cannot get on. He is on the bank—dying. My father!'

Then she burst into tears; and in the lantern light Ki saw the sparkling drops race down the smooth cheeks, saw them rise in the great eyes and overflow. He slowly removed the lantern handle from his teeth, and said—

'I cannot be plagued with you. I have other matters that concern me.'

He had been alarmed at first, fearing lest his encounter with Runham had been witnessed, lest this girl should be able to testify against him, were he taken to task for the death of his rival and adversary.

'Oh, come! Oh, do come!' sobbed Zita, as she grasped his boot more tightly.

'It was you who called?'

'Yes, it was I.'

'You called me?'

'Yes. There was no one else to call.'

'Oh,' said he, 'you saw no one else? No one with me?'

'No. I ran up the bank as you went by. I spoke to you, but you swore at me.'

'I—I did that?'

There was some mistake. She had taken him for the man now beneath the water.

'You shall not go!' cried the girl, clinging desperately to the stirrup. 'You cannot be so heartless as to let my poor father die.'

'What is your father to me? Let go.'

'I will not let go.'

He pricked his horse on, but she held to the bridle and arrested it.

'Take care!' said Drownlands. 'I will not be stayed against my will.'

She clung to the bridle.

'You may ride over me, and kill me too. I will not let go.'

'What do you mean?' asked he with a gasp. 'What do you mean by "kill me too"?'

'You shall ride over me, but I shall not let go.'

'But why did you say "kill me too"?' he asked threateningly.

'I will die as well as my father. I do not care to live if he die. How can you leave him? how can you be so cruel?' She broke forth into vehemence that shook her whole frame, and shook the horse whose bridle she grappled.

'What's that?' asked Drownlands, as the horse stumbled.

He held up the lantern.

On the embankment, under the horse's feet, lay the flail that had been twisted into his tiger-skin.

'I know you—I know you,' said the girl. 'It

was you who bought the flail.' Then again,
'My father is ill. He is sitting on the bank;
he cannot walk. He will die of the cold if you
do not help.'

'Let go,' shouted Drownlands, 'or I'll bring
the flail down on your hands.'

'You may break them. I will cling with my
teeth.'

He brandished the flail angrily.

Then Zita bowed herself, picked up the second
flail, and, planting herself across the way, said—

'You are bad and you are cruel. I cannot
get you to come to my father for the asking.
I will drive you to him—drive you with the
flail; I will force you to go.'

He tried to pass the girl, but she would not
budge; and before the whirling flapper and her
threatening attitude, the horse recoiled and
almost threw himself and his rider down the
embankment into the drove.

Drownlands uttered a curse, and again

attempted to push past, but was again driven
back by Zita.

'Take care, or I will ride you down,' he
threatened; then shivered, as he recalled how
that a few minutes previously Jake Runham
had used the same threat to him.

He considered a moment.

He could not allow this girl to retain the flail
she had picked up. It was evidence against
him. Every one in Burnt Fen, every one in
Weldenhall and Soham Fens, would hear of the
contest at Ely before the Cheap Jack van. If
that flail were known to have been found on the
embankment, it would be known at once where
it was that Runham fell into the Lark. It might
be surmised that a struggle had there taken
place, and marks of the struggle would be
looked for.

The girl who stood before Drownlands was
the sole person who could by any possibility
appear as witness against him—could prove

that he had been on the spot where Runham had perished ; and this girl was now appealing to him for help. It was advisable that she should be conciliated — be placed under an obligation to himself.

He made no further attempt to pass her ; he made no attempt to fulfil his threat that he would ride her down.

In a lowered tone he said, 'Where is your father ? '

'A little way back,' answered Zita. 'How far back I cannot say. I ran—I ran.'

'I will go with you. Give me up that flail.'

'No,' she answered ; 'I do not trust you. You would ride away when you had it.'

'I swear to you that I will not do that.'

She shook her head, retained the flail, slung it over her shoulder, and walked at his side.

Had she seen the contest ? Had she seen him beat his adversary down—down into the river? Drownlands asked himself these questions repeatedly, and was tempted to question her, but shrank from so doing lest he should awake suspicions. He need not have feared that. Her whole mind was occupied with a single thought —her dying father.

Drownlands riding, the Cheap Jack girl walking, retraced the path in the direction of Ely. Not for a moment would she relax her hold on the bridle, for she could not trust the good faith of the rider. The river was stealing by, the current so sluggish that it seemed hardly to move. It made no ripple on the bank, no lapping among the reeds. It had no curl of a smile on its face, no undulation on its bosom. It was a river that had gone to sleep, and was on the verge of the stagnation of death. Ki found himself wondering how far during the night the man and horse who had gone in would be swept down. He wondered whether it were possible that one or other had succeeded in making his way out. He had heard no sound; it was hardly possible that either could have escaped.

Presently a jerk on the reins roused Drown-lands from his meditations, and he felt his horse descend the bank, guided by the girl. In the darkness he could see a still darker object, which the faint light from a lantern on the bank partially illumined, along with a motionless horse, which seemed of very stubbornness to be transformed to wood. When, however, the beast heard the steps of its mistress, it turned its head and looked stonily towards her, with a peculiar curl of the nose and protrusion of the lower lip that was a declaration of determined resistance to being made to move forward. Zita paid no attention to the horse. She called to her father, and received a faint response.

'You will not leave me now? you will help? —you swear?' said she, turning to the rider.

'No,' answered Ki; 'now that I am here, I am at your service to do for you what I can.'

He dismounted and attached his horse by the bridle to the back of the van, then took one of his lanterns, and went to where he heard Zita speaking to her father.

'I be bad, Zit—bad—tremenjous. I be done for,' said the Cheap Jack. 'It's no good saying "Get along." I can't; there's the fact. I be stuck—just as the van be. I seems to have no wish but to be let alone and die slick off.'

'You shall not do that, father. Here is one of the gentlemen as bought the flails of us. He will help.'

Then Drownlands came to the side of the sick man and inquired, 'What is it? What can I do for you?'

'I don't know as I want nort,' answered the Cheap Jack; 'nort but to be let alone to die. Don't go and worrit me, that's all.'

'My farm is not a mile distant,' said Ki. 'Get into the waggon and drive along.'

'I can't abear the joggle,' answered the Cheap

Jack. 'I wants to go nowhere. But whatever will become of Jewel and Zit?'

He groaned, sighed, and turned over on the bank towards the scanty grass and short moss that covered the marl, and laid his face in that. The girl held his hand, and knelt by him. Presently he raised his head and said, 'Arter all, Zit, we did a fine business, what wi' the tea and what wi' the flails. Them as didn't cost us eighteenpence sold for one pun' thirteen and six —tremenjous!'

'Now listen to me,' said Drownlands. 'This horse of yours will never be able to get the van along. I will ride home and fetch a team, and we'll have the whole bag of tricks conveyed to Prickwillow in a jiffy. I'll bring help, and we'll lift you on to a feather tye.'

'You will not play me false?' asked Zita.

'Not I,' answered Ki, as he picked up the second flail; 'trust me. I shall be back in half an hour.'

He mounted his horse and rode away. The
girl watched him as he departed with some
anxiety; then, as he departed into the darkness,
Zita seated herself on the bank, and endeavoured
to raise her father, that his head might repose
on her bosom. He looked at her and put his
arm about her neck.

'You've been a good gal,' said he. 'You've
done your dooty to the wan and the 'oss and
me, and I bless you for it. That there tea as
we made out o' sweepins as we bought at
London Docks, and out o' blackthorn leaves as
we picked off the hedges and dried on the top
of the wan—'twas a fine notion, that. Go on as
I've taught you, Zit, and you'll make a Cheap
Jack o' the right sort. One pun' thirteen and
six for them flails! That's about one pun'
twelve profits. What's us sent into the world
for but to make profits? I've done my dooty
in it. I've made profits. I feel a sort o' in'ard
glow, just as if I wos a lantern wi' a candle in

me, when I thinks on it. One pun' twelve—I say, Zit, what's that per cent.? I can't calkerlate it now; it's gone from me. One pun' twelve is thirty-two. And thirty-two to one and an 'arf' —He heaved a long sigh. 'I be bad—I can't calkerlate no more.'

Zita leaned over the sick man's face, and with the corner of her gaily figured and coloured kerchief wiped his brow. His mind was wandering. From silence and impatience of being spoken to and having to exert himself to speak, he had come to talk, and talk much, in rambling strains.

'Father, I've brought you some brandy from the van. Take a drop. It may revive you.'

She put a flask to his lips. He found a difficulty in swallowing, and turned his face away. He had raised his head to the flask with an effort; it sank back on his daughter's bosom.

'Dad, how wet your hair is!'

'Things ain't as they ort to be,' said the Cheap

Jack sententiously. 'I've often turned the world over in my head and seed as the wrong side comes uppermost. Then I'm sure I was ordained to be a mimber o' parliament, but I never got a chance to rise to it. How I could ha' talked the electors over into believin' as black was white! How I could ha' made 'em a'most swallow anything and believe it was apricot jam! I could ha' told 'em lies enough to carry me to the top o' the poll by a thumping majority. It's lies does it, all the world over—leastways with the general public in England. It's lies sells damaged goods. It's lies as makes 'em turn their pockets out into your lap. It's lies as carries votes. It's lies as governs the land. The general public likes 'em. It loves 'em. They be as sweet and dear to the general public as thistles is to asses.'

Then he lay quiet, except only that he turned his head from side to side, as though looking at something.

I.—8

'What is it, dad?'

'I thinks as I sees 'em—miles and miles, going right away into nothing at all.'

'What, father?'

'The hawthorn hedges in full bloom, white as snow—it's our own tea plantation, Zit, you know — touched up wi' sweepins. When the flowers fall, then the leaves will come, and there'll be profits. Assam, Congou, Kaisow, Darjeeling, Souchong—just what you like—and, in truth, hawthorn leaves and sweepins—all alike. There's profits—profits comin' in the leaves, Zit.'

A light sleet was falling, and it gleamed in the radiance of the lantern planted on the bank near the dying man's head.

'So you see, Zit,' he said, pointing into space, 'the thorn leaves be fallin',—scores o' thousands, —and the green leaves will come and bring profits.'

'What you see is snow that is coming down, father.'

' No, Zit.   It's the thorns sheddin' their white flowers to grow profits.   Fall, fall, fall away, white leaves.'

He remained silent for a while, and then began to pluck at his daughter with the hand that clasped her waist.

' What is it, father ? '

' I ain't easy.'

' Shall I lift your head higher ? '

' 'Tain't that.   It's in my mind, Zit.'

' What troubles you, dad ? '

' That tin kettle wi' the hole in it.   I've never stopped it.   Put a bit o' cobbler's wax into the hole and some silverin' stuff over it, and you'll sell it quick off.   Nobody won't find out till they comes to bile water in it.'

' I'll do that, father.   Hush ! I hear the horses coming.'

' I don't want to go wi' them.   I hears singing.'

' It is the wind whistling.'

'No, Zit. It be the quiristers chanting in Ely. Do you hear their psalm?'

'No, we cannot hear them. They do not sing at night, and are also too distant.'

'But I does hear 'em singing beautiful, and this is the psalm they sing—"One pun' twelve—and hawthorn tea at four shillin'. There's profits."'

He was sinking. He weighed heavy on her bosom.

She stooped to his ear and whispered, 'Are you happy, father?'

'Happy? In course I be. One pun' twelve on them flails, and four shillin' on thorn leaves and sweepins—there's profits—profits—tremenjous!' And he spoke no more.

CHAPTER VIII

MARK RUNHAM

N O sight in the Fens is so solemn, so touching, as a funeral. There are no graveyards in the Fens. There is no earth to which
the dead can be committed—only peat, and this
in dry weather is converted into dust, and in rain
resolved into a quagmire. A body laid in it
would be exposed by the March winds, soddened
by the November rains.

Consequently the dead are conveyed, sometimes as many as nine miles, to the islets—to
Ely, to Stuntney, or to Littleport, wherever
there is a graveyard ; and a graveyard can only
be where there is an outcrop of blue clay. For
a funeral, the largest cornwain is brought forth,

and to it is harnessed a team of magnificent cart-horses, trimmed out with black favours.

In the waggon is placed the coffin, and round it on the wain-boards sit the mourners. The sorrowful journey takes long. The horses step along slowly, their unshod feet muffled in the dust or mire, and their tread is therefore noiseless. But their bells jingle, and now and then a sob breaks forth from one of the mourners.

Two waggons bearing dead men took the road to Ely. In one sat a single mourner, Zita ; and this waggon preceded the other. The second was full, and was followed by a train of labourers who had been in the service of the deceased, and of acquaintances who had roistered or dealt with him.

A cold wind piped over the level, and rustled the harsh dun leaves of the rushes in the dykes. Royston crows in sable and white stalked the fields, dressed as though they also were mourners, but were uninvited, and kept at

a distance from the train. Lines of black windmills radiated from every quarter of the heavens,
as though they were mourners coming over the
fens from the outermost limits to attend the
obsequies of a true son of the marshland.

To the south-west stood up the isle of Ely,
tufted with trees; and soaring above the trees,
now wan against a sombre cloud, then dark
against a shining sky, rose the mighty bulk of
the minster, its size enhanced by contrast with
the level uniformity of the country.

Although it cannot be said that no suspicion
of foul play was entertained relative to the
death of Jake Runham, yet nothing had trans-
pired at the coroner's inquest that could in any
way give it grounds on which to rest; nothing
that could in the smallest degree implicate
Drownlands.

Runham had drunk freely at the tavern at
Ely, and he had ridden away 'fresh' as a
witness euphemistically termed it, implying

that he was fuddled. He had started on his home journey with a single lantern, in itself likely to occasion an accident, for it vividly illumined one side of the way and unduly darkened the other. Some one in the tavern yard had commented on this, and had advised the extinction of the single light as more calcu-lated to mislead than none at all.

Horse and man had been discovered in the water about a mile above the drove that led to Crumbland, his farm. Runham had been found with his legs entangled in the stirrups. Possibly, had he been able to disengage himself when falling, he might have escaped to land. Cer-tainly the horse would have found its way out; but the weight of the rider had prevented the poor beast from reaching the bank. It was observed that Runham had gone into the canal on his right hand, and that the lantern had been slung to his left foot.

There were, it was noticed, contusions on the

head and body of the deceased, but these were easily accounted for without recourse to the supposition of violence. At intervals in the course of the Lark piles were driven into the banks to protect them against the lighters, and horse and man might have been carried by the stream, or in their struggles, against these stakes, and thus the abrasions of the skin and the bruises might have been produced.

Something was, indeed, said about a recent quarrel between the dead man and his neighbour, Drownlands ; but then, it was asked, when, for the last nineteen years, had there been an occasion on which they had met without quarrelling? The quarrel, according to report, had been inconsiderable, and had concerned nothing more than a flail for which both men had bidden high. Furthermore, Drownlands, it was ascertained, had been detained on his way to Prickwillow, before reaching the spot where the corpse had been found. He had been detained by the Cheap Jack's daughter on account of the Cheap Jack's sickness. It was known that Drownlands had summoned his men, and with a team of horses had removed the van to his rickyard. He had been attentive to the unfortunate vagabond, and had been at his side till his death.

There was no specifying the exact hour when Runham had fallen into the water, but, as far as could be judged, it must have been about the time when Drownlands was occupied with the Cheap Jack.

A floating suspicion that Ki might have had a hand in the death of Jake did exist, but there was nothing tangible on which a charge could be based. On the contrary, there was a great deal to show that he was not present ; enough to free him from suspicion.

When the funerals were over,—and both had taken place simultaneously, the graves being adjacent, one chaplain performing the service over both,—then the waggons returned. That in which the Cheap Jack's coffin had been conveyed to its last resting-place was empty. Zita declared her intention to walk.

Those who had walked behind the waggon of Runham were taken up into it, the horses started at a trot, and both conveyances were soon far away, and appeared as specks in the distance.

Zita walked slowly along the road. She was in no hurry. She had to resolve what she was to do for her maintenance.

Should she pursue the same trade as her father? Would it be safe for her to do so? At times there was a good deal of money in the van, and if she, a young girl, were alone, she might be robbed. She had abundance of ready wit, she had assurance, she had at command the stock-in-trade of old jokes used by her father, and was perfectly competent to sell goods and reap profits. But the purchase of the stock had been managed by her father, and with that part of the business she was not conversant. Could she manage the van and its stores and the horse alone? If not alone, then whom might she take into partnership with herself? Not another girl. A man it must be; but a man—that would not do for other reasons. The girl coloured as she walked and pondered on the perplexed question of her future.

She then considered whether it would be advisable for her to dispose of her van and its contents. But she saw that she could do so only at a ruinous loss. Her situation would be taken advantage of. The damaged goods would not sell at all, unhelped out in the exaggerations, lies, the flourish and scuffle of a public auction. All the articles were not, indeed, like the tin kettle and the ' own plantation tea.' Some were really good. A majority were good, but the collection was spiced with infirm and defective articles.

If she did dispose of the van and her stock,

what should she do with herself? Into service she could not go—the bondage would be intolerable. Into a school she could not go—she had no education. To become a dressmaker was not possible—she could not cut out. To enter a factory of any sort was hardly to be considered. She knew no trade. She could befool the general public—that was her sole accomplishment.

As she walked along, musing on her difficulties, she was caught up by a young man, dressed in deep mourning. At first he made as though he would pass her by, for he was walking at a greater pace than hers, but after a few steps in advance he halted, turned back, and said in a kind tone—

'We are both orphans. You lost your father on the same night as that on which I lost mine. They have been buried on the same day, and the same service has been read over both. I am Mark Runham; you are the Cheap Jack girl.'

'Yes, I am Cheap Jack Zita.'

'I could not call you by any other name ; your real name I did not know. Let us walk together, unless you desire to be alone.'

'Oh no.'

'When I was in the waggon, with my dead father in the coffin before me, I looked forward, and then I saw you—you, poor little thing, sitting alone, with your head bowed down over your father's coffin. I thought it infinitely sad. You were all alone, and I had so many with me.'

Zita turned her face to him.

'You are very kind,' she said.

'Not at all. My heart is sore because I have lost my father—but there is so much to take the sharpness off my pain ; I have my mother alive. And you ?'

'My mother has been dead these five years.'

'And I have many relatives, and more friends. But you ?'

'I have none. I am alone in the world.

'And then I have house and lands. And you?'

'I have the van.'

'A wandering house—no real house. What are you going to do with yourself?'

'That is just what I was considering as I walked along.'

'Will you tell me your plan?'

'I have none. I have not resolved what to do.'

'I am glad that I have caught you up. I sent on the waggon. I had to stay behind and make arrangements with the undertaker and the clerk. I am glad I remained; it has given me the opportunity of speaking with you. Our mutual losses make us fellows in sorrow, and you seem to me so piteously lonely. Even when I was in the wain my eyes wandered to you, and with my eyes went my thoughts. I could not fail to consider how much greater was your desolation than mine.'

Again Zita turned to look at the young fellow who spoke. He had fair hair, bright blue eyes, a fresh, pleasant face, frank and kindly.

' I think you sold something to my father,' he said ; ' I have heard the chaps talk about it. You sold it middling dear. A flail—and he paid a guinea for it.'

' Yes, I sold a flail for a guinea, and another for twelve and six. Mr. Drownlands bought one of them.'

' And my father the other. I was not at the fair when that took place, but folk have talked about it. I think, had I been there, I would have prevented my father bidding so high. The flail was not found with him when he was recovered from the river.

' No ; it was on the bank.'

' It was probably carried down by the Lark,' said he, not noticing her words, ' and went out in the Wash.'

The flail! Zita was surprised. One flail she

knew that Drownlands held when she met him, the other she had herself picked up, and had used to prevent him from continuing his course, and to compel him to assist her father.

She stood still and considered. The matter was, however, of no consequence, so she stepped on. If she found the flail at Prickwillow, she would take it to Crumbland. It belonged to Mark Runham by right.

'What is it?' asked the young man, surprised at her look of concentrated thought.

'It is nothing particular,' she answered; 'something occurred to me—that is all. But it is of no matter.'

'I should like to know what is going to become of you,' said the young man. 'Have you no kindred at all?'

'None that I know of.'

'And no home?'

'None, as I said, but the van. When that is sold, I shall have none at all.'

I.—9

'But you have friends?'

'A friend—yes—Jewel, the old horse. Well, he ain't so old, neither. I call him old because I love him.'

'I say, when you've made up your mind what to do with yourself, come to our farm, Crumbland, and tell me.'

'That's blazin' impudence,' said Zita. 'If you want to know, you can come and ask of me.'

'I cannot do that. Do you not know that my father and Ki Drownlands were mortal enemies? I cannot set foot on his soil, or he would prosecute me for trespass. If I went to his door, I would be met with something more than bad words.'

'Why were they enemies?'

'I do not know. They have been enemies as long as I can remember anything. Well, you will let me have some tidings concerning you. I will come out on the embankment near Prick-

willow, and you can come there too. It is so
dreadful that you should have no one to care
for you, and no place as a home to go to. If I
can help you in any way tell me. My mother
is most kind. As it has chanced that we have
both been made orphans at one time, and as
our two fathers were buried, as one may say,
together, and as we are walking home together,
it seems to me that it would be wrong and
heartless were I to do nothing for you. To sit
and nestle into my home and comforts at Crumbland and see you wander forth desolate and
alone—the Pharisee couldn't have done half so
bad with the poor man by the wayside, and I
won't. I should never forgive myself. I should
never forget the sight of the poor little lass in
black, with the coffin in the great waggon, all
alone.'

'You are kind,' said Zita, touched with the
honest, genuine feeling his tones expressed. 'I
thank you, but I want no help. I have money,

I have goods, I have a horse, and I have a home on wheels. And I have—what is best of all—a spirit that will carry me along.'

'Yes; but one little girl is a poor and feeble thing, and the world is very wide and very wicked, and terribly strong. I'd be sorry that this bold spirit of yours were crushed by it.'

'Here is the place where I live,' said Zita.

'Yes, that's Prickwillow drove. Here am I, eighteen years old, and I have never been along it—never been on Drownlands farm, along of this quarrel. And what it was all about, blessed if I or any one else knows!'

Zita lingered a moment at the branch of the road. Mark put out his hand, and she took it.

'I'll tell you what,' said she; 'you've been kind and well-meanin' with me, and I'll give you a milk-strainer or a blacking-brush, whichever you choose to have.'

Mark Runham was constrained to laugh.

'I'll tell you which it is to be next time we meet; to-morrow on the embankment — just here. Remember, if you are short of anything beside a milk-strainer or a blacking-brush—it is yours.'

CHAPTER IX

PRICKWILLOW

A SLEEPLESS night followed the day of the funeral. Zita needed rest, but obtained none. She had brain occupied by care as well as heart reduced by sorrow. She had loved her father, the sole being in the world to whom she could cling, her sole stay. The wandering life she had led prevented her contracting friendships. Since her father's death she had lain at night in the van. This conveyance was so contrived as to serve many purposes. It was a shop, a kitchen, a parlour, an eating-house, a carriage, a bank. The goods were neatly packed, and were packed so close that the inmates could very commodiously live in the midst of their stores. There was a little cooking stove in it. There were beds. There was, indeed, no table, but there were boxes that served as seats and as tables, and the lap is the natural dinner-table every man and woman is provided with.

When the front of the van was raised so as to shut up the shop for the night, the crimson plush curtains with their gold fringe and tassels concealed the board on which so much trade had been carried on during the day. There was a window at the back that admitted light. The stove gave out heat, and the inmates of the travelling shop settled themselves to their accounts, and then to rest.

The accounts were calculated not in a ledger, but on their fingers, and balanced not on paper but in their heads.

When darkness set in, then a lamp illumined the interior, and the little dwelling was suffused with a fragrance of fried onions and liver, or roast mutton chops—something appetising and well earned; something for which the public had that day paid, and paid through its nose. The horse had been attended to, and then the father sat on a bench, pipe in mouth and legs stretched out, and occasionally removed the pipe that he might inhale the fumes of the supper his daughter was preparing. Cheap Jack had possessed a fund of good spirits, and his good humour was never ruffled. He had been the kindest of fathers; never put out by a mishap, never depressed by a bad day's trade, never without his droll story, song, or joke. But for a fortnight before his death he had failed in cheeriness and flagged in conversation. The work of the day had become a burden instead of a pleasure, and had left him so weary that he could often not eat his supper or relish his pipe.

He had combated his declining health, and endeavoured to disguise the advance of disease, from the eyes of Zita. But love has keen sight, and she had noted with heartache his gradual failure of spirits and power. Till then no thought as to her own future had occupied her mind. Now that the dear father was gone, Zita had no one on whom to lean. No other head than her own would busy itself about her prospects, no other heart than her own concern itself about her to-morrow.

She was kindly treated at Prickwillow. The van was placed under cover, and the horse provided with a stall.

The housekeeper, a distant relative of Ki Drownlands, was hearty in her offers of assistance, and the maid-of-all-work, who was afflicted with St. Vitus' dance, nodded her kindly good wishes. Both Drownlands and the housekeeper had urged Zita to accept the accommodation of the house, in which were many rooms and beds, but she had declined the invitation; she was accustomed to van life, and could make herself comfortable in her wonted quarters. She needed little, and the van was supplied with most things that she required. There were in it even sufficient black odds and ends to serve her for mourning at her father's funeral. What was there not in the van? It was an epitome of the world, it was a universal mart, a Novgorod Fair sublimated to an essence.

'What are you about?' asked Drownlands.

He had come into the yard behind the farm-house, and he saw Zita engaged in harnessing the horse. The front was down, and on it stood a milk-strainer, some blacking-brushes, and a flail.

'What are you about? Whither are you going?'

Drownlands was a tall man, with a face like a hawk, and dark bushy brows that stood out over his eyes and the root of his nose.

'I am going,' answered Zita.

'Going? Who told you to go?'

'I am going to be an inconvenience no longer.'

'Who told you you were an inconvenience?'

'No one, but I know that I am not wanted.
I thank you for what you have done, and will
pay you.'

'Pay me?   Who said a word about payment?'

'No one, but of course I pay.   Mark Runham
—I think that was his name—was kind to me,
—that is to say, he spoke civil to me,—and I'm
going to pay him for good words with a milk-
strainer.   You have done me good deeds, and I
will pay you.   Get into the van and pick out
what you like up to five pounds.   Do you want
door-mats?   There's a roll o' carpet, but I don't
recommend it, and there's tinned goods.'

Drownlands stared at the girl.   Then his eyes
rested on the flail.

'What have you got that for?   It was in my
house.'

'Yes.   You took it in.   But it is not yours.
It belongs to Mark Runham.   His father bought
it of us.   He gave a guinea for it.   I picked it
up on the bank when I overtook you.   You had

your flail in your hand. You would have ridden on and left me and my father in the lurch, but I stood in the way with that flail. It is not mine. I have the guinea I received for it in my purse. Now that the old man is dead, for certain it belongs to his son. That is why I am taking it to him.'

'He shall not have it! He must not have it!' exclaimed Drownlands. 'How came you to know Mark Runham?'

'The young man walked from his father's funeral. So did I. He walked the fastest, and he caught me up. He spoke kindly, and so I shall pay him for it with a milk-strainer, or, if he prefers it, with blacking-brushes.'

'Give him the blacking - brushes, by all means.'

'Or the milk-strainer?'

'Or the milk-strainer; but not the flail.'

'It is his,' said Zita. 'The old man paid down his money for it.'

'Give him back the money, not the flail.
Here '—

Drownlands thrust his hand into his pocket,
and drew a handful of money, gold, silver, copper,
mixed, from it, and extended it to the girl.

' Here ! You said you would pay me for what
I have done. Pay me with the flail. I want
nothing more. Then I have the pair ; or if you
wish to restore the guinea—take it.'

' The flail was bought. It is no longer mine.'

Drownlands stamped, put out his hand and
snatched the flail from the board on which it
stood.

' He shall not have it. I will accept nothing
else.'

' Then I must give the young man its value
—a guinea's worth of goods.'

' Do so, and take the pay from me.'

' I will let him have your mats, and I'll tell
him that you '—

' Tell him nothing. Not a word about the

flail. That is all I ask of you. Say nothing.
If you owe me anything for what I have done
for your father and you, then pay me by your
silence.' He mused for a moment, then caught
the girl by the arm and drew her after him.
'Come and see all I have.'

He led her athwart the rickyard to where
were ranged his stacks of wheat—two, each
forty paces long, with a lane between them.
Down this lane he conducted her. 'Look,' said
he, 'did you ever see such ricks as these? No,
nowhere out of the Fens. Do you know how
much bread is in them? No, nor I. It would
take you many years to eat your way through
them ; and every year fresh wheat—as much as
this—grows. There are rats and mice in these
stacks. They sit therein and eat their fill, they
rear their families there. What odds is that to
me? A few more rats and mice—a few more
mouths in the house — I care not. There is
plenty for all.' Then he drew Zita into another

yard that was full of young stock, bullocks and heifers.

'Look here,' said he. 'Do you see all these? How much meat is on them? How long would it take you to eat them? Whilst you were eating, others would be coming — that is the way of Nature. Nature outstrips us; it shovels in with both hands, whilst we take out with one—so is it, anyhow, in the Fens. What is another cut off a round of beef to such as me?'

Then he strode to the stables, threw open the door, and said, 'There are stalls for horses; there is hay in the loft to feed them, oats in the bins to nourish them. What odds to me if there be one more horse in the stalls? Here!' he called to one of his men. 'Take the Cheap Jack horse out of the van-shafts again and bring him to this stable.'

Zita endeavoured to free herself from his grasp.

'No,' said Drownlands; 'you have not seen

all. You have been about the world, I dare-say; seen plenty of sights; but there is one thing you have not seen before, — a fen-farm, —and it is a sight to unseal your eyes. Come along with me.'

He held her wrist with the grip of a vice, and now drew her in the direction of the kitchen.

'Look!' said he. 'What is that? That is our fuel. That is turf. What do we pay for keeping ourselves warm in winter? Nothing. I have heard say that some folks pay a pound and even forty shillings for a ton of sea-coal. And for wood they will pay a guinea a load. We pay nothing. The fuel lies under our feet. We take off a spit of earth, and there it is for the digging, some ten—fifteen—twenty feet of it. It costs us no more than the labour of taking up. Do I want a bit of brass? I go to market, and say I have ten acres of turf to sell at sixty pounds an acre. A dozen hands are held up. I get six hundred pounds at once. That is what I call making money. Come on. You have not seen all yet.'

He drew her farther. He pulled her up the steps to the door, then turned, and, pointing to a large field in which were mounds of clay at short intervals, he said—

'Do you see that? What is done elsewhere when land is hungry, and demands a dressing? Lime is brought to fertilise the exhausted soil. We in the Fens never spend a shilling thus. If we desire dressing, we dig under the turf, and there it lies — rich, fat clay—and spread that over the surface. That is what it is to have a fen-farm. Come within now.'

He conducted Zita through the door, and threw open the dairy.

'Look,' said he. 'See the milk, the churns, the butter. Everything comes to us in the Fens. Butter is a shilling a pound, and there are twenty-eight pounds there now. There will

I.—10

be as much next churning, and all goes as fast
as made. Touch that churn. Every time you
work it you churn money. Come on with me
farther.'

He made the girl ascend the stairs, and as he
went along the passage at the head of the stair-
case, he threw open door after door.

'Look in. There are many rooms; not half
of them are occupied, but all are furnished.
Why should I stint furniture? I have money
—money! See!' He drew her into a small
apartment, where were desk and table and
chairs. It was his office. He unlocked a safe
in the wall.

'See! I have money here—all gold. Come
to the window.'

Drownlands threw open the casement. Below
was the yard, in which were the young cattle,
trampling on straw and treading it into mire.
He thrust his hand into his pocket, drew forth
a handful of coins, and, without looking what

he held,—whether gold, or silver, or copper,—
he threw it broadcast over the bullocks and
heifers. Some coins struck the backs of the
beasts, and bounded off them and fell among
the straw, some went down into the mud, and
was kneaded in by their feet.

'What is money to me? It grows, it forces
itself on me, and I know not what to do with
it. I can throw it away to free myself of the
trash and more comes. It comes faster than I
can use it; faster than I can cast it away. Now,
girl—Cheap Jack girl—now you know what a
fen-farm is. Now you see what a fen-tiger
can do. You remain at Prickwillow with me.
I will shelter you, feed you, clothe you, care for
you. Eat, drink, sleep, laugh, and play. Work
a little. All is given to you ungrudgingly.'

He put the flail to his knee and endeavoured
to break it, but failed. Then he cast it into the
corner of the room, where was a collection of
whips, sticks, and tools.

'There,' said he, 'all I ask is—not a word about my having been on the embankment. Not a word about the flail—least of all to Runham. I have my reasons, which you do not understand, and which you need not know.'

Zita hesitated. She had not expected such an offer. She doubted whether she could contentedly settle into farm life.

'You were about to leave,' continued Drownlands, 'or rather to try to leave. But how could that horse of yours draw the van out of the Fens? You know how it was when you came this way. The wheels sank, and the horse was powerless. I sent my team, and only so could we draw the van along. Never, unassisted, could you reach Littleport or Ely, not, at all events, in winter. When you got into the drove the wheels would sink again, and I should send my team and drag the van back here once more. You have got your feet into the peat earth and clay, and are held fast. Listen to me.

Supposing you did get a little way and then stick, and I were angry at your departure, and refused to come to your aid and draw you back to Prickwillow, what then? Let me tell you what would happen were you left out all night unprotected, sunk to the axle in the fen. There are slodgers in the fen; there are tigers, as they call them here—plenty round Littleport. That story of the sale of the flails is spread and talked about. It is known that you have money. It is known that your father is dead. Do you think there are not men who, for the sake of what money you have, would not scruple to steal on you in the dark, to come up like rats out of the dykes, like foxes from the holes, and take your money, and nip that brown throat of yours to prevent peaching? If you think there are not, then you think differently of the Fens and the fen-men than do I who have lived in the Fens and among the tigers all my days. Come'—

He put his hand to her throat and pinched it.

'This, and your body found in a drain, black in fen-water, of a morning. This on one side; on the other, my offer of a home, protection—everything.'

Zita withdrew from his grasp with a shudder.

'I accept your offer,' she said; 'I can do no other. There is no choice in the matter.'

'You are right there,' said he, with a laugh. 'To you there is no choice.'

CHAPTER X

RED WINGS

DAYS passed; Zita had settled into Prick-willow. She was given her own room, and into that she removed the contents of the van. The walls were lined with the stock in trade, and the crimson and gold curtains festooned the window.

A chamber in a farmhouse seemed to Zita bare and comfortless after the well-covered interior of the shop on wheels. She could not rest till she had hidden the naked walls, and brought her room into some resemblance to the interior of the rolling house she had inhabited for so many years. But she had further reasons for accumulating the stores in her own apartment. The van was in an outhouse, and was exposed to damp, with its attendant evils, moth, rust, and mildew, that would make havoc of her property if exposed to them.

Zita made herself useful in the house. She considered that she could not accept the offer made her of shelter and sustenance without acknowledgment of a practical nature, and as she was endowed with energy and intelligence, she speedily adapted herself to the work of a farmhouse. She found that there was need for her hand. The housekeeper was without system, and disposed to abandon to the morrow whatever did not exact immediate attention. The maid with St. Vitus' dance was a worker, but required direction. Zita had been compelled to be tidy through the exigencies of van life. In the travelling shop a vast number of very various goods had to be packed into a small compass, and the claims of trade had obliged her to keep every article in the brightest con-

dition, that it might look its best, and sell—
if possible — for more than its intrinsic value.
Accordingly, not only did Zita see that everything was in its place, but also that everything
was furbished to its brightest. She was nimble
with her fingers in plying the needle, and took
in hand the household linen, hemmed the sheets,
attached buttons, darned holes, and put into
condition all that was previously neglected, and
through neglect had become ragged, and was
falling to premature decomposition.

The girl noticed that Drownlands watched
her at her work, but she also saw that he
averted his eyes the moment she gave token
that she perceived his observation ; she was
aware, not only that she interested him, but
that he, in a manner and in a measure, feared
her.

She had a difficult course to steer with Leehanna Tunkiss, the housekeeper, who had received the tidings that Zita was to become an

inmate of the house for some length of time, with doubt, if not disapproval. The woman, moreover, resented the improvements made by the girl as so many insults offered to herself. To hem what had been left ragged was to proclaim to Drownlands and to the quaking helpmaid, that Lechanna had neglected her duty ; to sew on a button that had been off the master's coat for a week, was to exhibit a consideration of his interests superior to her own.

At the outset, before the funeral, the woman had been gracious, believing that Zita was but a temporary lodger. When she found that she was likely to become a permanent resident, her manner towards her completely altered.

One afternoon, when Zita had nothing particular to engage her, she wandered along the drove, and then rambled from it across the fields.

A frost had set in on the day of her father's funeral, and had ever since held the earth in fetters. It was one of those severe frosts that so often arrive in November, and sweep away the last traces of summer, clear the trees of the lingering leaves, and then sere the grass that is still green.

It was one of those early frosts which frequently prove as severe as any that come with the New Year. The clods and the ruts of the drove were rigid as iron. It would have been difficult to move the van when the way was a slough, it was impossible now that it was congealed. The lumps and the depressions were such as no springs could stand, and no goods endure. Pots would be shivered to atoms, and pans be battered out of shape. Whatever Zita may have desired, perhaps hoped, she recognised the impossibility of leaving her present quarters under existing circumstances. A thaw must relax the soil, harrows and rollers must be brought over the road, before a wheeled conveyance could pass over it. Finding it difficult, painful even, to walk in the drove, where there was not a level surface on which the foot could be planted, Zita deserted it for a field, and then struck across country towards a mill, the sails of which, of ochre-red, were revolving rapidly. The fields are divided, one from another, by lanes of water. The fen-men all leap, and pass from field to field by bounds —sometimes making use of leaping - poles. With these latter they can clear not the ditches only, but the broad drains or loads.

Zita was curious to see a mill. From one point she counted thirty-six, stretching away in lines to the horizon. She had hitherto known windmills only for grinding corn. Here the number was too considerable, and their dimensions too inconsiderable, for such a purpose.

Lightly leaping the dykes, she made her way towards the red-winged mill. As she approached, she saw that the mill was larger than the rest, that it had a tuft of willows growing beside it, and that, on an elevated brick platform, whereon it was planted, stood as well a small house, constructed, like the mill, of boards, and tarred. This habitation was a single storey high, and consisted, apparently, of one room.

On the approach of Zita, a black dog, standing on the platform with head projected, began to bark threateningly. Zita drew near notwithstanding, as the brute did not run at her, but contented itself with protecting the platform, access to which it was prepared to dispute.

Then Zita exclaimed, 'What, Wolf! Don't you know me? Haven't you been cheap-jacking with us for a couple of months, since father took you off the knife-swallowing man? We'd have kept you, old boy, but didn't want to have to pay tax for you, so sold you, Wolf.'

The dog had not at first recognised Zita in her black frock ; now, at the sound of her voice, it bounded to her and fawned on her.

A girl now came out from the habitation,

called, 'What is it, Wolf?' and stood at the head of the steps that led to her habitation, awaiting Zita.

'Who are you?' asked the girl on the platform. She was a sturdy, handsome young woman, with fair hair, that blew about her forehead in the strong east wind. Over the back of her head was a blue kerchief tied under her chin, restraining the bulk of her hair, but leaving the front strands to be tossed and played with by the breeze. She was, in fact, that Kainie whose acquaintance we have already made.

'I believe that I know who you are,' she said.

She had folded her arms, and was contemplating her visitor from the vantage-ground of the brick pedestal that sustained mill and cot. 'You are the Cheap Jack girl, I suppose?'

'Yes. I am Cheap Jack Zita. And who are you?'

'I—I was christened Kerenhappuch, but some folks call me Kainie and Kenappuch.

I answer to all three names. It's no odds to
me which is used.   What do you want here?'

' I have come to look at the mill.   What is its
purpose ?   You do not grind corn ? '

' Grind corn ?   You're a zany.   No ; we
drive the water up out of the dykes into the
drains.   Come and see.   Why, heart alive !
where have you been ?   What a fool you must
be not to know what a mill is for !   Step up.
Wolf won't bite now he has recognised you.
If you'd been some one else, and tried to step up
here, and me not given the word to lie still, he'd
have made ribbons of you.'   She waved her
arms towards the low wooden habitation.   ' I
lives there, I does, and so did my mother afore
me.   Some one must mind the mill, and a
woman comes cheaper than a man.   Besides,
it ain't enough work for a man, and when a
man hasn't got enough work, why, he takes to
smoking and drinking.   We women is different ;
we does knitting and washing.   We's superior

animals in that way, we is. Here I am a stick-at-home. I go nowhere. I have to mind the mill. You are a rambler and a roll-about—never in one place. It's curious our coming to know one another. What is your name, did you say?'

'Zita—Cheap Jack Zita.'

'Zita? That's short enough. No wonder with such a name you're blowed about light as a feather. It'd take a thundering gale to send Kerenhappuch flying along over the face of the land. Her name is enough to weight her. Now, what do you want to see? Where does your ignorance begin?'

'It begins in plain blank. I know nothing about mills.'

'My mill is Red Wings. If you look along the line to Mildenhall and count ten, then you'll see Black Wings. Count eight more, and you have White Wings.'

The girl threw open a door and entered the

fabric of the mill, stepping over a board set edgewise. She was followed by Zita.

Nothing could be conceived more simple, nothing more practical, than the mechanism of the mill. The sails set a mighty axletree in motion, that ran the height of the fabric, and this beam in its revolution turned a wheel at the bottom, that made a paddle revolve outside the mill. This paddle was encased in a box of boards, and at first Zita could not understand the purpose of the mechanism, not seeing the paddle.

'Would you like to climb?' asked Kainic. 'Look! I go up like a squirrel. You had best not attempt it. If your skirts were to catch in the cogs there'd be minced Cheap Jack for Wolf's supper. I'm not afraid. My skirts seem to know not to go near the wheels, but yours haven't the same intelligence in them. A woman's clothes gets to know her ways. Mine, I daresay, 'd be terrible puzzled in that van of yours.'

I.—11

'Don't you talk to me about petticoats,' said Zita. 'Petticoats to a woman is what whiskers is to a cat. They have feeling in them. A cat never knocked over nothing with his whiskers, nor does a woman with her skirts if she ain't a weaker fool than a cat.'

Then up the interior of the mill ran Kainie, with wondrous agility, playing in the framework, whilst the huge axletree turned, and the oak fangs threatened to catch or drag her into the machinery.

'Do come down,' said Zita. 'I do not like to see you there.'

But it was in vain that she called; her voice was drowned in the rush of the sails, the grinding of the cogs, and the creak of the wooden building.

Presently Kainie descended, as rapidly as she had run up the ribs of the mill.

'Mother did not let me do it when she was alive,' said the mill girl. 'But I did it all

the same. Now, what next? Come and see
this.'

She led Zita outside, and took her to the
paddle-box, flung open a door in it, and exposed
the wheel that was throwing the water from the
'dyke' up an incline into the 'load' at a con-
siderably higher level.

'It licks up the water just like Wolf, only it
don't swallow it. There's the difference. And
Wolf takes a little, and stops when he's had
enough; but this goes on, and its tongue is
never dry.'

'Does the mill work night and day?'

'That depends. When there's no wind, then
it works neither night nor day, but goes to sleep.
But when there has been a lot of rain, and the
fen is all of a soak—why, then, old Red Wings
can't go fast enough or long enough to please
the Commissioners. Look here; the water has
gone down eighteen inches in the dyke since
this morning. Red Wings has done it. He's

not a bad sort of a chap. He don't take much looking after. There's a lot of difference in mills; some are crabbed and fidgety, and some are sly and lazy. Some work on honest and straight without much looking after, others are never doing their work unless you stand over them and give them jaw. It's just the same with Christians.'

'And what is that long pole for?' asked Zita.

'That, Miss Ignorance, is the clog. I can stop the wings from going round if I handle that, or I can set the sails flying when I lift the clog. Come here. I'll teach you how to manage it.' She instructed Zita in the use of the clog. 'There!' said she; 'now you can start the mill as well as I can, or you can stop it just the same. You've learned something from me to-day. I hope you won't forget it.'

'No; I never forget what I am taught.'

'Not that it will be of any use to you,' said

Kainie. 'You're never like to want to set a mill going.'

'Perhaps not; but I know how to do that, and it is something. There is no telling whether I may want it or not.'

'It's as easy as giving a whack to the hoss who draws the van,' said Kainie.

'Now,' said Kainie, after a pause, 'this here hoss of mine has reins too. Do you see those two long poles, one on either side, reaching to his head? Them's the reins ; with them I turn his head about so that he may face the wind. That's the only way in which my hoss can go. Now come and see where I live.'

She led the way to her habitation, which was beyond the sweep of the wings.

'It's small, but cosy,' said Kerenhappuch. 'No one can interfere with me, for Wolf keeps guard. But, bless you, who'd trouble me? I've no money. And yet one does feel queer after such things as have happened.'

'What things?'

'Ah! and it is a wonder to me how you or any one can abide in the same house with him.'

'With whom?'

'Why, with Ki Drownlands. Though he be my uncle, I say it.' The girl's face darkened. 'He never spoke to my mother, his own sister; never helped her with his gold, and he rich and we poor. The Commissioners gave us our place, not Uncle Drownlands.'

'Who are the Commissioners?'

'You are a silly not to know. Every man who owns a couple of score acres in the Fens is a Commissioner. And the Commissioners manage the draining, and levy the rates. They have their gangers, their bankers, their millers —I'm one of their millers. No,' said Kainie vehemently. 'No thanks to Ki Drownlands for that.' She grasped Zita by the shoulders, put her mouth to her ear, and said in a half whisper, 'It was Uncle Ki who killed Jake Runham.'

Zita drew back and stared at her.

'I am sure of it,' said Kainie ; 'and there be others as think so too, but durstn't say it. But there is nothing hid that shall not come to light. Some day it will be said openly, and known to all, that Ki Drownlands did it.'

CHAPTER XI

TIGER-HAIR

ZITA walked back in the direction of Prick-willow with a weight on her heart and her mind ill at ease. Incidents half observed rose in her memory and demanded consideration—as in a pool sunken leaves will rise after a lapse of time and float on the surface. Facts that had been indistinctly seen and scarce regarded, now assumed shape and significance.

She recalled the incidents of the night of her father's death, and marshalled them in order with that nicety and precision that marked her arrangement of the goods in the van. She remembered how that she had seen two men ride along the bank, one after another, with an interval of some minutes intervening between them, as they passed above where she had been with the van and her father. The first rider had been furnished with two lanterns to his feet. She had let him pass without attempting to arrest him. That man she now knew was Hezekiah Drownlands. Then, after a lapse of some minutes, a second rider had passed, going in the same direction. He had carried a single lantern attached to his left stirrup. To him she had run, him she had brought to a standstill, and she had asked and been refused his assistance. That man was Jeremiah Runham.

Zita next recalled every particular of the run along the bank after the second rider. She now distinctly remembered having seen a glitter of several lights before her, a cluster of lights leaping and falling, flashing and disappearing. How many these had been she could not recall. They had changed position, they were not all

visible at once. At the time, in her distress of
mind, she had not counted them. But she was
now convinced that the lights which she had
seen, and seen in one constellation, had been
more than two. A single star would have
represented Runham. Two stars would have
indicated Drownlands. More than two—that
showed that the men had been together.
Further, she had heard shouts and cries. At
the time, as she ran, she had supposed that
these were in response to her appeals for assistance; but when she had reached Drownlands,
the only man on the bank she did come upon,
then, as she now recalled, he was startled at her
appearance, as if it were wholly unexpected.
He could not, therefore, have called in answer
to her cries. But where was the third light?
What had become of Runham?

When she had reached Drownlands no third
light was visible, whereas a minute previously
there had certainly been more than two

before her. What had become of the second rider?

It was, of course, conceivable at the time that the third light had been extinguished, and the second rider was in full career along the bank in the direction he desired to go. But such an explanation was no longer admissible when it was known that this rider was dead, and had been drowned in the river. When Zita considered that this rider, Runham, had been found in the water, with the light of life as well as that of his lantern extinguished, and when she remembered that she had picked up the flail he had been carrying at the spot where she came up with Drownlands, it appeared certain to her that Drownlands must have witnessed, if he did not cause, the death of Runham. It was possible that Runham, returning tipsy from market, may have urged his horse on one side, so as to pass the man before him, and so have plunged into the river; and it was possible enough that Drownlands had chosen to maintain silence on the matter, lest any admissions on his part might have been construed into an accusation of having caused the death of his adversary.

Zita was turning these thoughts over in her mind when she reached the embankment. She started to walk along it. She was confident that she could fix the spot where she had slipped into the water, and that was but about a hundred paces from where she had come up with Drownlands. She remembered to have observed there a post in the water that had in it a mortice-hole, like an eye, and that the head was so indented and rugged as at one moment to make her suppose it was a human face.

As has already been stated, there had been sufficient frost to harden mud into rock. Traces of a scuffle—if a scuffle had taken place—would be recognisable still to an eye that knew precisely where to look for them.

Zita went with nimble feet, a busy brain, and fluttering heart towards the point where the van had been arrested in the mud, and she resolved thence to follow the course she had taken on that eventful night along the bank. On this occasion she walked deliberately where she had previously run, and came after a while to the spot where, according to her calculation, she had slipped into the canal. There she found the post standing up out of the water to which she had clung, close to the bank, with the mortice-hole in it that had looked so like a human eye. This was the only post of the kind she had come across, and this was not more than a hundred yards from the spot where she had grasped Drownlands' foot, had held him, and had heard him scream at her touch.

At this point, some hundred yards beyond the post with the hole in it, she carefully explored the soil. The top of the embankment was indented with hoof-marks, but these might have

been made by the gangers' horses, which were
constantly driven up and down the embankment. But there was something that satisfied
the girl that at this spot a struggle had taken
place, for on the land side of the embankment
tufts of grass and clods of clay had been torn
out and thrown into the drove, and on the water
side hoof-marks and a slide in the greasy marl
were sealed up by the frost as evidences of a
horse having there gone down into the water.
These had not been observed by any one else, as
no one save Zita had known the exact place
where to look for them, and though distinguish-
able enough when searched for, they were not
obtrusively manifest.

Zita had not merely a well-arranged mind,
but she was able to prize whatever facts came
before her at their true value.

Now, as she walked away from the river towards Prickwillow, she realised that there was
strong presumptive evidence that Drownlands

had been engaged in a tussle with his enemy,
and that he knew how it was that Runham had
met his death, even if he were not absolutely
his murderer.

As Zita entered the house, she heard the
master's voice raised in tones of anger. He
was addressing Mrs. Tunkiss, the housekeeper.

'It's all idle excuse—you don't want the
trouble of it. I know your ways.'

'I haven't a needle will go through it,'
answered Leehanna.

Then Drownlands came out of the kitchen.
He was swinging in his hand the tiger-skin that
usually in cold or wet weather was slung over
his shoulders. His eye lighted on Zita, and his
face brightened at once.

'Look here, you Cheap Jack girl,' said he.
'The servants are idle curs, both of them. I
want Leehanna Tunkiss to mend my skin. I
have torn it. A few threads will suffice, and she

declares she has no needle that will go through the leather. It's all idleness and excuse.'

'I will do it,' said Zita. 'We have all sizes and sorts of needles in stock—for cobblers, tailors, and all.'

She took the tiger-hide out of his hand.

'That's my greatcoat — my mantle by day and my rug and coverlet by night,' said Drownlands. 'I wear no other. We, who have been born and bred in the Fens, folk are pleased to call fen-tigers. That is why I got this skin. Ten, fifteen years ago it was for sale in Ely, and I bought it as a fancy, and have come to think I can't do without it. Folks have got to know me now by it, and call me the Fen-tiger King. Can you mend it?'

Turning the skin about, Zita said, 'It has been given a wrench—tremenjous.'

'Well, so it has, and there is a rip as well. If it is not drawn together now, it will go worse. I don't want to wear rags, and I won't, that's more — though Lechanna would have me, to save trouble. It is easier to find an excuse than to run threads with a needle.'

' I will do it,' said Zita. ' But you must suffer me to take it to my room, that I may find a suitable needle and stout thread.'

' Yes, take it,' said Drownlands, with his beetling brows drawn together and his eyes fixed on her from below them. ' Yes, Chestnut-hair! you can do everything. In your store you keep everything but excuses.'

'We could not sell them,' said Zita.

' And it is with excuses Lechanna serves me,' he replied, and looked sideways angrily at his housekeeper, who retreated muttering into the kitchen.

Then Drownlands went out, and Zita retired to her room to accomplish the task she had undertaken. As she turned the hide about, she was struck with the evidence it gave of having been wrenched and twisted with great strain of violence. The wrench was no ordinary one, produced by the catching of the skin in a nail or door. The hide was in one place stretched out of shape by the force exerted on it; not only so, but it had been contorted. Again, on closer investigation, it appeared that some of the hair had been ripped out by the roots, by this means exposing the bare hide.

As Zita worked at the repair, her busy brain occupied itself with the causes of this strain and rent: how they could have been produced, why the tension had been so excessive.

That Drownlands had not ridden to Ely on the fair-day with his skin torn she was convinced by his asking to have it mended now; whereas, had it been in this condition before fair-day, he would have required it to be repaired before riding into Ely. Drownlands was eccentric in his dress, but he was also punctilious about its neatness. The injury done to the tiger-skin must have been done since Tawdry fair-day. All at once Zita dropped needle and twine, started up, left her room, and went to that which Drownlands used as his office, the apartment into which he had conducted her when he showed her his money.

Into the corner of this room he had flung the flail that he had taken from her when she was about to leave his farm and to return it to Mark Runham; the flail she had picked up on the bank was that Runham the elder had bought from her for a guinea.

Zita knew that Drownlands was out, she had seen him go to the stables across the yard. He had not returned. She had not heard his voice or step in the house since. Into the office she was justified in penetrating, for the master had asked her to keep it in order for him. Lechanna Tunkiss neglected it, on the excuse that she was afraid of disarranging his papers and books. Zita knew that both flails were in this room; that which Drownlands had bought was suspended to a nail, the other was in the corner where he had cast it.

Zita took both flails and examined them. She saw that they had been subjected to rough usage. The wood was bruised in both. It had not been so when they left her hands in the afternoon of Tawdry Fair. The flappers were dinted, and there was a deep bruise in the 'handfast' of one. Both had been employed to strike, and both had clashed against each other.

Zita replaced Drownlands' flail on the nail whence she had unhitched it, and took a further look at that which had belonged to Runham.

She now observed that the leather thongs that attached the flapper to the handfast were twisted, stretched, and strained, and that in the twist was a tuft of hair precisely similar to that of the tiger-skin.

She detached some of this hair, took it to her room, and compared it with that still in place on the hide. There could no longer be any question but that a struggle had taken place between the two men, that they had fought with the flails, that in course of the contest the flail of Runham had become entangled in the hide worn by Drownlands, and that the flail had been twisted, and so had strained and torn the skin.

In this case Drownlands most certainly knew of the death of his adversary, and had had some hand in it.

Zita knew enough, and she shuddered at the thought that she was enjoying the hospitality of a murderer.

CHAPTER XII

ON BONE RUNNERS

'HEIGH! Cheap Jack girl!'

Zita was out enjoying the crisp, frosty air, on the frozen soil, sparkling under the winter sun.

The November frost had continued, and canals and rivers were iced over as well as dykes and drains. God's plough was in the soil—that is what country folk say when the frost cuts deep into the earth. Where God's plough has been, there golden harvests are turned up to gladden all sorts and conditions of men, and golden harvests turn to metallic gold in the pockets of the farmers.

Every fen man, woman, and child can skate.

As soon as a child has found its legs, it essays to slide, and when it can slide, it attempts to skate. Fen skating is inelegant. Speed alone is considered, and legs and arms fly about in all directions. With scorn does the fen-man contemplate the figuring of the fine gentleman on the ice.

In winter, skating matches come as thick as do football matches elsewhere. Parish is pitted against parish, fen against fen, islet contests with islet; even the frequenters of one tavern are matched against the frequenters of another.

During a hard frost, locomotion for once becomes easy and speedy in the Fens. Men and women skate to market, children to school, and smugglers run their goods from King's Lynn.

Zita had gone to the river side to see a sight that was novel to her. As she stood watching the skaters, Mark Runham came to the bank side, his cheeks glowing, his fair hair blowing about his ears, his eyes sparkling as though frost crystals were in them.

'I say, Cheap Jack, get on your patines and come.'   Skates are termed *patines* in the Fens.

'If you mean skates, I have none. Besides, I do not know how to use them.'

'Not got patines?   Not know how to use them?   Then take a ride in my sleigh. I'll run you along. Stay here a few minutes till I have brought it.'

He was gone, flying down the river like a swallow, and in ten minutes he had returned, drawing after him a little sledge, and stayed his course on the frozen surface of the Lark before Zita.

'It's fine fun,' said he, with a voice cheery as his smile. 'I'll run you where you like to go ; to Rossall Pits if you will—to Littleport—down to the sea—up to Cambridge—to the end of the world—anywhere you will.'

'Take me for a short distance only.'

'Then seat yourself in the sledge. We shall
go as the wind.'

Zita descended the bank to the ice.

'Look!' said he ; 'do you see how my sleigh
is made ? It is set on the leg-bones of a horse.
It runs on them in prime style. They wear as
steel, and slip along better.'

With her face radiant with happiness, Zita
placed herself in the little sleigh.

Then with a merry 'Whoop!' off he started
down the river. The wind rushed in Zita's face,
sharp and fresh, and drove the blood to her
cheeks.

They passed many 'patiners,' men and boys.
There were few women out. Later, when the
sun set, they would skate along the frozen
surface to the tavern. The tavern is an institu-
tion in the Fens more frequented than elsewhere,
and frequented without scruple, not by men
only, but by women as well. There is a reason
for this. The fen-water is undrinkable. There

are no springs in the Fens. Those who live near
the rivers derive thence their tea water; river
water is potable and harmless when boiled, that
which is drawn from the peat is neither. Consequently the inhabitants of the Fens are compelled to drink something other than water,
and instinctively seek that something other at
the public-houses. When the woman's work-
day is over, she dons her patines and is off to
the 'Fish and Duck,' or the 'Spade and Becket,'
the 'Pike and Eel,' or the 'Sedge Sheaf,' to
moisten her dust-dry clay.

As Zita flew along the ice, she laughed for
joy of heart. Never had she travelled so fast.
Her wonted pace had been that of the snail,
for she had made progress in a heavily-laden
van, drawn by a depressed and stolid horse.
She was whirled past one of the main pumps
for throwing the water of the loads into the
river, and before she conceived it possible, she
had passed a second. And these engines, as

Mark told her, were two miles apart. Jewel's fashion of travelling was very different from that of Mark. Along the smoothest and most level road he had been accustomed to crawl, and then, after having made his pulses throb and his sweat break out, to stand still, with head down, to revive himself. Then nothing would induce him to proceed till he considered himself refreshed, when he would stumble on for a couple of miles, and again pause. But Mark flew along as though he would never know exhaustion, and there was no bringing him to a standstill.

After several vain attempts to arrest him, Zita succeeded. He stood beside her sleigh with a smile on his pleasant face, and with the steam blowing from his nostrils.

'You must not go too far,' said Zita. 'We have come a long way from Prickwillow.'

'What! are you tired? You have not been dancing on sketches?'

'I do not understand your meaning.'

'Sketches?—does that word puzzle you as did patines? They are what some folk call stilts. I can run on them like a crane. But sketches are cumbrous, and, when the fen is soft, tire one speedily.'

'Let us return now.'

'No indeed. You have nothing to call you back. That fellow Drownlands, old scoundrel, —I beg your pardon,—will not be angry with you and thrash you, I suppose?'

'He is not at home. He has gone abroad for the day.'

'Then come along. We will visit Newport.'

'Please do not take me much farther.'

'Why not? Are you not enjoying the run?'

'I love it.'

'Then away we go. You are not afraid of travelling, with me as your horse?'

She looked straight into his bright, honest

face, and laughed. 'No—you are too good for any one to fear you.'

'How do you know that?'

'You carry honesty in your eyes, and "good boy" written across your brow.'

'It is time for me to run,' laughed Mark, 'or my head will be turned.'

He buckled himself to his task, pranced from side to side, swinging the little sleigh to right and left, in his light-hearted frolic, and then away he went, running the sleigh with Zita in it straight along the canal.

The flatness, the monotony of the Fens, the absence of unshackled nature, the treelessness of the region, the lack of everything that can arrest the changing lights and passing shadows, combine to make the district one to send a chill into the mind of the visitor. Flat as the sea, it is devoid of its diversity of tint and tumultuous or glassy beauty. Nevertheless, the fen exercises a charm over the mind and holds with a spell the heart of the native. He can live nowhere else. He will not emigrate. He feels bound to spend all his days in the fen. Only when the vital spark expires does his body leave the turf to repose in the clay of the islet graveyards. That the farmer and landowner should love the fen is not marvellous, because of the richness of the soil and the profits they make out of it; but why the labourer should cling to the spongy turf is not so explicable. He may be discontented, and be a grumbler, but he is discontented with his lot, and envies the taverner or the smuggler on the Fens, grumbles at the hardness of his work or the lowness of his pay; but he is not discontented because the fen is so flat, and he has no word against its hideousness, or, at least, its uniformity.

One reason why the labourer in the Fens does not think of leaving it may be that he uses tools there different from those employed elsewhere, and he would have to learn his trade anew,

employ unfamiliar tools, and be subjected to
ridicule when handling them awkwardly. It is
strange, but true, that those men are more
naturally prone to leave their homes who
inhabit mountainous lands than such as dwell
in level districts.

How far was Mark going? How Zita flashed
past the windmills, some of which had their
sails in motion! A little rising ground showed,
with some trees clustered on it—that must be
Littleport.

'Mark,' said Zita suddenly, 'I want to ask
you a question.'

'Say on,' said he, and relaxed the speed at
which he was spinning her along, and finally
came to a standstill. How pretty she was, with
her glowing cheeks, her cherry lips, the light of
the winter sun in her soft hazel eyes and in her
rich, burnished, chestnut hair! How pretty
that hair was now, in some confusion, puffed
out of its order, the coppery strands on her brow,

one down her cheek! The wildness of her
appearance thus untidied by the wind made
her more than ever charming.

Mark looked with eyes that could not be
satiated with looking.

But it was not merely her beauty that struck
him. It was the exuberant happiness that
seemed to be bursting forth at her eyes, running
out of her little head in every shining hair,
glowing in those bright-tinted cheeks, burning
in those carnation-red lips.

'Well, my dear little Zita, what is it?'

'Mark, it is something I have thought about
and have puzzled over. It seems strange to
speak about it now—now when I am so joyous
—and it is connected with things so sad to me
and to you.'

'But what is it, little rogue?'

'Mark, that terrible night when your father
and mine died'— She paused.

'Well, Zita?'

'Then—before his death, I mean—before the death of my own dear daddy, and I can't say whether it was before or after yours was drowned —I heard such a strange, such an awful sound.'

'Where?'

'In the sky—above; like the barking of dogs. It was just as though a hunter was going by with his pack. Shall I tell you what I thought it? It was just as if the dogs had smelt the fox, and gave tongue. Was it not dreadful? I could see nothing; I could hear—that was all.'

'I think nothing of that,' said Mark. 'I know our fen-folk say it is the devils running after a human soul. They have snuffed it from the bottomless pit, then the Great Hunter of Souls opens the kennel door, and out they burst, yelping, snapping, panting, and come after it.'

'Oh, Mark!'

'But if the soul be very nimble, it runs before them, runs on the wind, swift as an arrow, and

I.—13

slips in at heaven's gate, and then the evil spirits yelp and bay and bark outside. But it is all fudge and nonsense. I believe that the sound comes from the wild geese.'

'I shall ever think of this. Oh, I hope I shall never hear that dreadful sound again. My dear father—no—he would certainly escape those hounds. They would never catch him. For him the Golden Gate would be opened, and the dogs be shut outside. He was so gentle, so kind, so true. Oh, I loved him so—so much!' And thereupon the brightness was gone out of the sunny little face, and it was bathed in tears.

'Put all this aside. Think no more of it.'

'They were in full pursuit when I heard them.'

'The geese? And you are a little goose if you think more of this.'

'Mark, may I never hear that sound again!'

'Or, if you do, Zita, may I be near you to

laugh your fears away. No, not laugh—kiss them away, as I do now.'

'Mark! you *are* a naughty boy! I did not think it of you.'

The roses had come back, and the glow was returned, and in one cheek deeper than the other.

CHAPTER XIII

PIP BEAMISH

'DO go on and leave me alone,' said Zita.

Then again the young man sped forward with the sledge, at full speed on his skates. There was a glow of something more than health—something more than the reaction produced by the fresh wind in his cheeks.

'Here's a joke!' exclaimed Mark, stopping for a moment. 'I see quite a throng round Beamish's mill.'

Again he went on. And Zita, looking in the direction he had indicated, saw that a considerable number of persons was collected, some on the banks, some on the ice, and as many as could be accommodated on the brick platform of a windmill.

Without halting, Mark said, 'The paddle can't go because of the frost, but Pip Beamish's tongue can wag, and when it wags it is for mischief. He is a restless, dissatisfied rascal. We'll go and hear what he has to say.'

Mark stayed the sledge when he reached the outer ring of the congregation that was gathered together about the mill.

The day was Sunday, so no work was being done. There were idlers everywhere, specially on the ice. In present days there is little church-going in the Fens, in former days there was none. Churches are few and far apart. In mediæval times the monks of Ely had chapels on every islet that rose a few feet above the meres, and they boated from one to another, gathering around them for divine service and moral instruction the aquatic population of the Fens. With the Reformation these chapels were let fall into ruin, and care for the souls of the fen-dwellers ceased. The canons of the cathedral were wealthy and idle, and it never so much as occurred to their sleepy, stagnant consciences that they had duties to perform towards the inhabitants of the district whence they drew their revenues.

When the meres were dried, and settlers occupied the drained land, then the parochial clergy were unable to cope with the altered condition of affairs. The roads were impassable, the distances enormous, their incomes had not increased with the alteration in the value of the lands included in their vast parishes. Consequently, the fen-folk came to think little of their religious duties. The church towers might serve as landmarks, but the church pastors were not spiritual guides. The only form of religion that commended itself to an amphibious population was Anabaptism, and that mainly because it consisted of a good

souse in fen-water. A few of the sterner spirits
settled into the sect, but the bulk of the natives
grew up and lived without any religion at all;
or, if they professed to be Christians, they took
care to allow it in no way to interfere with their
profits or their pleasures.

The assemblage about the mill consisted of
labouring men and their wives; some were in
their Sunday clothes, but others had not taken
the trouble to 'clean' themselves. Such were
the men who lounged about on holidays with
springes and nets in their pockets, and a gun
barrel up the left sleeve.

A stool was planted close to the mill, and on
it stood a young man with high cheek-bones,
long dark hair, and glittering eyes under heavy,
bushy brows. He had unusually lengthy arms,
and at the extremities of the arms unusually
broad, flat hands. These he flourished about.
He drew in his elbows to his sides, and em-
phasised an appeal by suddenly throwing out

his arms and extending his fingers. Having his back to the mill, which was constructed of boards, what he said was audible to some distance. The boards served as reverberators.

'I say it is a sin,' shouted the orator. 'Here be the farmers turning earth into corn, and corn into gold guineas, and the men as helps them to do it ain't paid enough to keep body and soul together. What was wheat a quarter only a short while ago? It was one hundred and twenty shillings and sixpence. Now it is ninety-six shillings. And what are the wages? Seven to ten shillings. What is the difference between seven shillings and ninety-six? Eighty-nine, is it not? That is what goes into the farmers' pockets. Who do all the work? And who get all the gains? Look into every stackyard and see what wheat is there for the rats and mice to eat,—they are not begrudged it, let them eat,—but you and your children must starve. Why are not the stacks threshed out? Because the farmers are waiting till the wheat goes up to one hundred and twenty-six shillings again. You may perish of hunger—that is nothing to them. Your children may run naked—that is nothing to them. You may drink fen-water because you haven't twopence to pay for a half-pint of beer—that is nothing to them. You mayn't have a blanket to throw over your beds this freezing weather—they don't care. You may have the walls of your cots so full of cracks that the wind whistles through them—they don't care. Your hands have held the plough, your hands have sown the corn, your wives and children have hoed it three times, you have reaped it, you have stacked it—and there it stands for rats and mice to eat, till prices go up to one hundred and twenty-six shillings. Ninety-six is not good enough for them,—these bloodsuckers,—and you are content to let things remain so. What I maintain is, that you have a right to say to the farmers,

"Thresh out now while we are hungry; the price is too high even now for us, and why should sad days for us be golden days for you?"'

His address was received with applause.

Mark turned to Zita and said in a low tone, 'He is right after a fashion. I'll set to work and thresh to-morrow. I'll let the labourers who are on my farm have this corn ten per cent. under market price. I cannot act fairer than that.'

'And how is it with the millers?' pursued the orator. 'Don't they take toll of every sack of corn you send to them to be ground? Are not their pigs and cows kept fat on what the miller's fist brings up out of your flour? As if it were not enough that you were cheated by the farmer, you must be cheated also by the miller. Pillaged in every way, pinched on every side, trodden on by every one—that is your fate.'

His words met with applause.

'We have gone on hoping, and we have been
disappointed. What good comes to us from
Parliament? None at all. What help do we
get from the laws? The laws are made for the
benefit of the farmer, and not for the poor man.
What good to us are magistrates — justices of
the peace? They are appointed to hold us
down, to fine and imprison us. They are the
farmer's friends, not the friends of the poor
man. We are told that Old Boney is the foe
of our country. Men are called from the
plough, plucked away from their wives and
children, to serve the king against this Bona-
parte. What does patriotism mean? It means
loving the country where we are ill-treated and
starved, loving the king who never concerns
himself about us, loving the laws that oppress
us, loving the magistrates who imprison us,
loving the farmers who are sucking the marrow
out of our bones. I'm no patriot. As well ask
a poor prisoner to love his jail, shed his blood

in its defence. I'll tell you what it is, friends, Heaven helps them who help themselves. No good will come to us from waiting. Heaven is silent so long as we bear and do nothing, but Heaven will send its lightning and hailstones when we take the matter into our own hands. It was so in the day of battle in Gibeon ; then the Lord cast down great stones from heaven upon the oppressors of Israel, and made sun and moon to stand still **till** they were cut to pieces, smitten hip and thigh. The great stones would have remained in the clouds, sun and moon have taken their usual courses, had not Joshua and Israel armed themselves to fight— to right their own wrongs. So will it be again, so has it ever been, so will it be unto the end. We must raise our hands to fight our fight, raise our hands against our oppressors, or there will be no help for us from on high. If you remain hoping and doing nothing, then, as I said before —to be trampled into the mud—that is your fate.'

'And to be thrashed and to be kicked out of employ — that is what is laid up for you, you rascal!' shouted an imperious voice.

Zita and Mark looked round, and saw behind them Drownlands on his horse.

'I will see to you, Pip Beamish, as sure as that I am a Commissioner,' continued the master of Prickwillow. 'You were not set to tend a mill that you might stump it and foment ill-feeling. I shall report what you have said at the next meeting of the Commissioners, and shall have you cast adrift.' Then, turning to the audience, Drownlands brandished his whip and cried, 'As for the rest of you, disperse instantly, or I will ride up and down among you and lash you with my whip, and send you skipping home.'

The crowd broke up into knots, then further dissolved and dispersed.

'I'll have your names, and see that you are

thrown out of employ. Get home at once, before the whip is at your breech.'

The haughty, commanding tone of the man, and the knowledge that he was one ready to execute his threats, seemed to make those who hesitated consider that the better part of valour was discretion, and they scattered in all directions.

Drownlands, upright in his stirrups, looked about him, marking those who seemed reluctant to obey his orders. Then his eye rested on Zita. His face changed immediately.

'You here?'

'Mark ran me up in his sleigh.'

'Mark? Mark? What Mark? How dare you come here without leave from me?'

'I am not your servant. I am not your prisoner. I go where I choose. I do what I will,' answered Zita, nettled at his tone.

'Hallo!' scoffed Drownlands. 'What! has the mad folly of Ephraim Beamish infected your little brain?'

' My brain is sound enough. It is you, Master Drownlands, who forget what your place is, and what is mine. You are not my master. I am not your servant. I pay my way. I am a lodger at Prickwillow, nothing more. If I please to go out for a run on the ice with Mark, I am not idle. I have done my work in your house, and may enjoy myself as I like.'

' Do not bandy words with me.'

' It is of no use arguing with him,' whispered the young yeoman. ' He is in one of his passions, when he acts and talks unreasonably. Take no notice of him.'

' What are you whispering about? Making mock of me?' roared Drownlands.

' Come, Cheap Jack,' said Mark, ' jump on to the sleigh again; and you, Master Drownlands,' he looked at the horseman with a laugh, ' let us race—you on the bank, I on the canal—and Zita the prize.'

END OF VOL. I.